SKELETONS

in the

SWIMMIN' HOLE

Tales from Haunted Disney World

KRISTI PETERSEN SCHOONOVER

Monorail Clear

Casey's brother had died while clutching a Magic Kingdom ticket.

Casey kept the ticket under a refrigerator magnet so he'd see it every night before he went to his job as a monorail pilot; Saturday, though, he notices it's missing.

At work, he locks up the monorail fleet for the evening and starts hurrying to his car, only to stop when he hears the *whoosh* of a train on a nearby beam.

"I know I secured them," he says on a call to his supervisor. "Should I go back and investigate? Someone could be joyriding."

"No one told you?" his boss replied. "We have special hours for guests who held non-expiring tickets at death."

ISBN: 978-0-615-40280-2

Cover art and interior design by Millennial Concepts. Published in the United States, October, 2010.

The fonts used in this book are from the Goudy Old Style BT font family.

Admit One Literary Theme Park Press
249 Great Plain Road
Danbury, CT 06811
www.haunteddisneytales.com
admitonepress@gmail.com

For Nathan
When the going gets tough, the tough go to Disney World.
October, 2009

"Miss Reyna Gets Her Comeuppance on Flash Mountain" first appeared in *Scalped* Issue 2, Fall, 2009. www.scalpedmagazine.com.

"Romancing the Goat" first appeared in *The Oddville Press* Volume 1, Issue 5, October, 2009. www.theoddvillepress.com.

"Charlotte's Family Tree" first appeared in *A Fly in Amber*, November, 2009. wwwaflyinamber.net.

TABLE *of* CONTENTS

Doing Blue

I'm at a Christmas Eve Loaves and Fishes party and we were required to come dressed as food items.

Magda is decked out as a side order of French fries and just as I'm thinking her costume's pretty cool, she looks me up and down with disapproval, particularly at the backs of my legs. Then she leans over the bean dip and says, "I don't see any track marks, Livvie. When was the last time *you* did it?"

The stereo blasts a Dixieland version of "Joy to the World" as Roger comes around the corner. He's dressed as Jesus, only since he seriously believes he is Jesus, he's really not in costume. We work at this religious theme park called Bible Country and I'm his—well, bodyguard or assistant or whatever you call it. I dress as the Virgin Mary and make sure when he poses for photos with people he doesn't get inappropriately fondled, begged for miracles, or pelted with rocks.

The mention of track marks at a party thrown by Jesus freaks me out. "Last time I did what?" I have a hard time shoving a chip in my mouth. Because I had decided to come as a milkshake, the giant straw made of wrapping paper tubes taped to my spine makes it hard for me to feed myself.

Magda shoots a confused expression in Jesus' direction. "Blue," she says. "*Nobody* at this party isn't doing blue. Right, Jesus?"

"It is my hope that we can show Livvie here

that life is more than food, and, like, the body is more than clothes." Jesus' long white sleeve drags through the bean dip as he reaches for the plate of Oreos.

She looks shocked. "You mean you invited someone who's never done it? Are you out of your *mind?*"

"Blessed are the poor in spirit, man, for theirs is the Kingdom of Heaven." Jesus picks up an Oreo, closes his eyes, bows his head, and moves his lips soundlessly.

"That's okay," I say. "I…I don't do drugs."

My sister Tara did drugs to the point where I couldn't stand going to her house. It was just so filthy, dishes and dirt and junk everyplace, dust so thick it changed the color of the countertop. And don't even think about crashing over on the couch.

"I'm all good, chicken, why worry? They make me happy," Tara used to say.

Hell, I didn't need drugs to be happy. I *was* happy up North. And I am happy, I guess, living down here, working at Bible Country. Although I really don't have a choice. Nobody from up North knows where I am. I just had to take off one day and leave everything, and I can't say it doesn't haunt me. I'm afraid of my phone, people from my past finding me. The last couple of weeks I've been hearing my phone ring only to find out it hadn't rung at all. I was hearing things.

One of the cardboard fries on Magda's costume falls out and lands in a bowl of Fritos. She selects a chip and keeps her lips parted when she bites down, showing all of her teeth, white and perfect except for one incisor that's cocked at an odd angle. "It's not a drug. Well, not *really*. If you've been to Disney World, you've probably done it."

Here in Winter Garden just two blocks from the Liki Tiki Lagoon Water Park, we're seven miles from Disney's main gate. Everybody around here assumes you've been to Disney World.

I never have. Not because I hate Disney or anything. It's more because…well, unless you're Jesus, you don't get paid too much more than eight bucks an hour.

"Blue. As in Blue Line." Magda reaches for the bottle of wine on the kitchen island and a couple more of her cardboard fries fall like bird droppings into various bowls of food. "You know, the TTA. The Tomorrowland Transit Authority. Used to be called the WEDWay Peoplemover. That elevated tram. With the cars and the blue vinyl seats, the one that goes all around Tomorrowland." She uncorks the wine and fills her glass. "It's quite a rush. You get on a magical escalator and it brings you to a place of white arches and pylons. You sit in a booth and lie back against the cool seats and when the train starts moving, there's a breeze and a rhythmic pulsing you feel in your thighs. You smell gas near the Indy Speedway and cooked onions from the Space Dog cart. You forget *everything*. Every wrong in your life is righted. You walk away a new person."

For a moment, this is tempting, for there is so

much I want to forget. Back in Rhode Island, I was a church secretary and bookkeeper, a damn good one, too. I could type faster than bottles of wine empty at Christmas parties and was especially brilliant in helping distraught families organize funeral proceedings five minutes before the casket was supposed to be carried in. Only thing was, I wasn't so good with money—I never had quite enough to help people out. Let's face it, being a church secretary may get you into heaven but it's not going to get you into a Millionaire's Club.

For the first few years nobody noticed I was touching up the books. I'd send my cousin three hundred bucks so she could pay the vet's bill after her cat swallowed a bunch of elastic bands or cover my friend Maureen's car payment. I justified this by telling myself religion was about helping those in need.

And I could've kept doing it if Tara hadn't done so many drugs.

One day I went to her house and she was staring at the wall, combing the cat with what she *thought* was a pet brush but was really just an orange popsicle. That's when I had to do something. I put her into a very expensive rehab center courtesy of St. Peter's Church. Which turned out wasn't as easy to justify. And wasn't as easy to hide.

So I took off for Florida. And here I am.

"Man," Jesus says, "Doing Blue is like a thousand epiphanies. You go into this euphoric state and you're at peace. So you can feel all the things you are and all the things you'll eventually be, man. Clarity." He picks up a pumpernickel cube, plows it through the spinach dip, and holds it up to my mouth. "My body, which is broken for you."

I'm not sure what to do so I just look at the cube. A blob of dip falls on the kitchen island.

"I thought I was the only one who got communion," Magda snaps.

This makes me uncomfortable; I'd only accepted Jesus' invitation in the hopes of making a few friends. The last thing I want to do is piss off the girl who might have something holy going on with my host. So I don't open my mouth. Instead, I say, "No, it's cool. I'm full."

Jesus frowns. "Come on, Livvie. You know, only the righteous can, like, enter the kingdom of heaven."

Ha! I am obviously far from righteous. Oh, I hope every day Tara is doing better. Sometimes I imagine our first phone chat in over a year. Initially the fantasy's totally pleasant, all about how she's clean now, she lives in a nice apartment, she's got a good job.

But then the fantasy deteriorates. Tara will say "Deacon Bob is looking for you, crazy looking for you, determined to find you. Was something going on with you guys?" Oh, yes, I'll have to explain, there was something going on between Deacon Bob, kind Deacon Bob, nice Deacon Bob and me, alright. Deacon Bob probably had to explain to the church that thousands of dollars were missing; I have nightmares about him before a scowling tribunal, his black sideburns gray from stress, his deep-set eyes bloodshot from lack of sleep. He was probably defrocked because of me.

Or, worse, she'll say, "Deacon Bob told me what you did, and I just can't live with that. For your own good, I told him where you are and he's on his way." They'll march into Bible Country and whether or not I'm all Virgin-Mary'd up they'll escort me onto one of those white prison buses that only goes one way.

Pick an outcome. Cream or sugar, I'm going to hell.

Jesus is still holding the bread out for me, but he doesn't look puzzled that I haven't taken it; he looks—I don't know, almost sympathetic. Another blob of dip falls, but this time it misses the kitchen island and lands on the floor.

Magda's glare is so hot it's making me itch, but Jesus' eyes are the most startling blue, a shade south of Tahitian, and I feel my mouth opening, my eyes closing, the cold bread sponge in my mouth.

When I open my eyes, Jesus is gone.

Magda says something.

I blink. "What?"

"I said, Livvie, short for Olivia, right?"

"Yeah." Which is actually my middle name. I started going by it when I moved here in the hopes it would intensify the smokescreen.

"I'm trying to be…polite?" She slides the bowl of shrimp toward her and roots through it with her fingers. "That Jesus and I…his routine is really only for me. Do you understand?"

I want to say *no, I don't,* because Jesus is… Jesus. One day Jesus told me about his how father had gone into diabetic shock, but there was nothing in the house to give him. "I just, like, prayed," Jesus said, "and when I opened the refrigerator, there was juice there. Where before, there had been none. And I knew then that the world would see greater things than that." The day after he told me that story, it was so skin-searing hot they closed Bible Country at ten in the morning, and me and Jesus went to a water park. I spent most of the day convincing him not to make a scene by attempting to turn the Lazy River into wine.

"Veins," Magda says, looking me squarely in the eyes and holding out a shrimp. "I warned Jesus to be careful when he was deveining. Half of these still have little black pieces in their backs. You know what they say about eating the vein. It's poison." She picks out a piece of vein and smears it on the countertop. She bites the shrimp in half.

There's a commotion at the slider.

"It's Jesus," says a hyperventilating tomato. "He's down."

Magda drops the shrimp and rushes outside, and when I follow I see the mass of people dressed as food parting. Jesus is in the center, on the ground, his body splayed in the shape of a cross.

Magda tries to kneel down to comfort him, but her French fry outfit won't let her. She does an

I'm-on-hot-coals dance. "Get this thing off me! Undo my zipper, for God's sake."

A spinach tortellini steps out of the crowd and helps pull the fabric and foam off her arms. She sheds the costume and is now only in a white leotard with red stripes on the sleeve and collar.

"I…am…thirsty," Jesus gasps.

"Get him some apple juice," Magda pleads.

I look at Jesus.

And standing over him, staring and pointing his finger at me, is Deacon Bob. And, just like I'd imagined, *his sideburns are gray.*

I hear myself scream because *dear God he found me how did he get here has Jesus known him all this time and I didn't know and what do I do now…*

"Apple juice!" Magda's cry is startling.

Deacon Bob has vanished.

"I'll…I'll get it." Feeling shaky, I go into the house, passing a chicken wing and a strawberry making out on the living room couch to the tune of Frank Sinatra singing "Silent Night."

The kitchen counter is strewn with used paper plates, their designs marred by shrimp tails and blobs of onion dip. I brace myself against the counter and try to breathe. I did *not* just see Deacon Bob. I'm seeing things, that's all. All this talk about Doing Blue. I got spooked.

I grab a plastic cup, throw a couple of ice cubes in it, and fill it from a bottle of apple juice that's sitting on the counter. I peer out the window which overlooks the lawn by the pool.

Deacon Bob's face is in the window.

"Go away!" I shout. "Get out of here!"

Chicken Wing and Strawberry get up off the couch and run.

Bob is gone again. I see Jesus, still on the ground, Magda cradling his head in her lap.

On the way back outside I snag a paper towel, because maybe Jesus won't be able to lift his head to drink. I hope he can go to work tomorrow. If he's out of a job, then, technically, so am I.

"Here, Jesus," Magda says, dipping the paper towel into the cup and moistening his lips. "Juice."

Jesus flaps his mouth. It reminds me of a fish on a hook.

"You didn't take your insulin, did you?" Magda says. "You know better."

"I was like," Jesus mouths, "way too busy preparing the house for…Livvie."

Oh, no.

Magda's eyes are black stones. "Really."

"She needs…blue," he murmurs.

Murmuring among the restless food: *blue, blue, blue!*, breathy, creepy—something out of a George Romero movie.

Magda has one of those toxic smiles, one of those I-just-got-you-disinherited smiles. "The Magic Kingdom is probably closed by now, it's Christmas Eve."

"No," Jesus says, "the Kingdom is open until 2:00."

The curious faces around me—a pepperoni,

a dish of spaghetti, a meatball—wait in silence. A martini scratches the back of one of her thighs. The hum of the pool filter is the only sound. Well, that and the distant strains of some song about ice in heaven I've never heard before playing on the stereo.

This is insane.

"Really, I…I have to go." I turn my back on Jesus and Magda and start walking toward the sunroom slider.

And standing on the other side of it is Deacon Bob. I close my eyes. "You're not real," I hiss through clenched teeth. "You're not."

But when I open them, he's still there.

In front of me, my past; in back of me, my future. I remember what Jesus said in the kitchen, *it is, like, a thousand epiphanies…you can feel all the things you are and all the things you'll eventually be.* "I'll go," I say. "I'll go, I'll go." After all, they said it makes all of your problems go away, and obviously Deacon Bob is a problem, so he'll go away.

I turn and see Magda helping Jesus to his feet; he holds out his arms. "I have risen, man." He looks directly at me. "We will go now to the Kingdom."

The restless food items chant *blue, blue, blue* as they strip out of their costumes and in a few minutes the lawn is Goliath's version of Bible Country after the crowds have gone—covered in giant litter. They walk past Jesus and nod respectfully and I hear cars starting up in the driveway.

Magda's eyes burn mine. "I'll be watching you." She pushes past me and into the house.

"I tell you the truth, man." Jesus sets his hand on my shoulder and his body heat is intense. "Today you will be with me in, like, paradise."

* * *

Magic Kingdom's Main Street hurtles me to Christmas Eve when I was eight. Small white lights grace every roof. Cookies and candy are everywhere and it's okay to eat them all day long. Colorful window displays remind me to put that Barbie Dream House on my list. I feel something I haven't felt in a long time.

Excitement.

Though I don't know why. There aren't any presents or even a tree waiting for me back in my apartment, and Jesus and I both have to work tomorrow because it's Bible Country's busiest day of the year.

People are staring at us, which probably has something to do with the fact that a guy dressed up as Jesus is leading a silent flock on a beeline toward Tomorrowland. We get up near the castle, where a Christmas tree covered with miniature Mickey Mice flashes from white to blue. A heavy older woman in Sunday clothes stops Jesus. "Oh, may I have my photo with you, sir?"

This is what rings Jesus' bells. He welcomes her by his side and the woman's equally-elderly friend snaps pictures with one of those throw-away cameras.

The crowd of former food we've brought

with us stands there, glassy-eyed, some of them looking desperately toward the neon morass that is Tomorrowland. Many of them are scratching the backs of their thighs.

"We need to go," Magda says. She frowns at me. "Why don't you go do your job?"

But I don't move, because suddenly a gaggle of geezers has formed a line, and a man in a priest's collar brings up the rear.

Deacon Bob. Who strides toward me with purpose, his eyes blazing.

I scream and duck behind Magda, who murmurs "Jesus Christ" before she confronts the priest and I'm left feeling naked as an adolescent in the gym shower. Just as I duck behind someone else in the crowd of former food, I see the priest *isn't* Deacon Bob.

"We're sorry, but Jesus needs to go cure a leper now." Magda snits as she grabs Jesus' arm.

The line collectively whines, but the priest takes charge. "Come on, ladies, we'll need to go over to Fantasyland now if we want to ride the Pooh thing before we have to line up for the fireworks!"

I think I see a splinter of recognition in the priest's eyes. I look down at my feet.

Jesus takes my hand. "Come," he says.

Magda fumes, but I stop being upset about her as we pass over a bridge and into corridors of neon. It's Vegas for ten-year-olds, children posing with people dressed as blue creatures and Michelin men with wings.

DOING BLUE

We are at the gates: TOMORROWLAND TRANSIT AUTHORITY, and Jesus guides me to an escalator belt that ascends to a square of light. From above, an echoing, disembodied voice encourages people to *stay clear of the doors and enjoy the trip aboard the Metroliner!*

When we reach the top, we follow a labyrinth of sleek silver railings to another moving platform hugged by blue trains, which look like five or six connected diner booths. There is the sound of elevator chimes and a female voice warns us about stepping onto the moving platform and remaining seated. A woman in a short gray dress with a name tag that reads SARAH smiles and ushers us to a booth. I take my seat across from Jesus and move over to make room for Magda, but when she tries to board, Jesus holds up his hand. "Give us some space. You cannot go where we're going."

Magda reacts with a poisonous scowl, and I suck in a breath, thinking *here comes the cat fight!* But she says nothing and boards the booth behind ours. The rest of the crowd of former food doesn't get on our train. They wait until the train behind us moves up on the conveyor belt.

The disembodied voice lets us know we are *"departing for a round trip Super Skyway Tour!"* and the train begins to move, really move: *THUMP bump rump rump rump rump,* the sound tires make on asphalt. We cruise past white pillars every few feet.

I look back at Magda in the car behind us. She is staring toward me, but not at me. Her eyes are glassy.

We are at the same height as tree tops, and below us, bug-sized people meander through pools of fluorescent light. We pass above a shop sign that reads *Merchant of Venus* and the disembodied voice tells us about a new convention center *"for all your out-of-this-world gatherings!"* There are ambrosial smells, hot dogs and popcorn, angelic strains of a synthesizer version of "White Christmas", a cool breeze. And suddenly I feel as though I'm part of the vehicle, at one with this great sinuous blue ribbon. It's like I've just slipped into a warm bath, like I've put my feet up after a long day, like oatmeal on a sunburn, ice cream on a sore throat. Magda, Deacon Bob, Jesus, the rent due next week, it all melts off me. I let the metronomic bumping lull me to happy places: swimming in the apartment complex pool on a really hot day. Shopping after-Christmas sales. The week off that Bible Country owes me. I was thinking of going to the community college to sign up for some classes, in what I don't know, but I could go see what they have. I am seized by the idea that I could do anything, anything I wanted. When I get done Doing Blue I could run out of here and call a taxi and have it drive me all the way to New Mexico. Or I could move to Key West and live on the beach. Maybe I can paint! I've always wanted to paint. I can ditch the past and I can ditch the job at Bible Country and I can—

This is Doing Blue, all the things you are and all the things you'll eventually be. I'm floating, and the last time I felt this much at peace was when I used to sit in the back of St. Peter's and listen to the vespers.

I have found it. I have reached Heaven. As close to Heaven as I know I will ever get.

A hard bump and a shift to the right brings me out of it. We are back at the boarding station. I look at Jesus, and he nods at me with a self-satisfied smile.

SARAH looks down upon us and asks us if we'd like to go again. And of course, we do. And each time we return to our point of departure, I have envisioned myself doing such exciting things, I want more. So we go on another ride-around. Again. And again. And again.

It is our seventh ride-through when I feel something on the backs of my thighs, a furious sting-itch. What the hell? I lean back against the seat, lift my right leg, strain my neck to get a look.

Spidery red veins course down the back of my thigh and pool in an angry bruise in the dimple behind my knee.

Track marks. The track marks Magda had been looking for. Caused by sitting bare-legged on the vinyl seats for so long.

And suddenly Deacon Bob is sitting across from me, wearing the same complacent smile I've seen on bodies at wakes. It's not just his sideburns that are gray now, but *all* of his hair. Then he breaks into a grin and I see he is missing his two front teeth, and one incisor is coffee-colored. *OhmyGodOhmyGodOhmyGod.* I stand up and try to get away from him, pressing back against my seat. But we're in a moving vehicle a hundred feet in the air. We bank around a corner and I almost pitch out of the booth.

"Get the hell away from me!" It occurs to me that such an attack might not be strong enough. On TV when they need to make evil things go away they're a hell of a lot more severe than that. "Get thee back, devil!"

Jesus frowns, puzzled. He looks in the seat next to him.

"Don't you see him?"

Jesus shrugs. "My eyes see like, nothing, man."

But Deacon Bob's knee is pressing against Jesus'. "You don't see him? Right there! Next to you! A man in black!"

Jesus doesn't have time to answer because Deacon Bob reaches out his long-fingered hand and makes to seize me.

That's it. Height or no height. I'm getting out of this booth. I start to climb out, over the back and into the booth behind us, but a frigid hand seizes my ankle and tugs. "Stop!" I'm yelling. "Stop!" Searing in the joint of my hip. *Deacon Bob is going to pull my leg from the socket.* "Stop!"

"My lord! You'll be killed!" That's Magda. Screaming from the car in back of us, her hair blowing around her like a thicket of thorns.

"What?"

"Not you!" she shrieks. "Jesus!"

And Jesus yells: "There is no greater than a

guy who would lay down his life for his friends, man!"

Confused, I twist my upper body around. There is no Deacon Bob. Deacon Bob is gone, and it is Jesus who has his hand on my ankle. There is a look in his eyes I've seen before, the look that was in Tara's eyes the day I dropped her off at the rehab center, the look in her eyes when she said to me, *how could you do this to me? I thought you were my sister.*

"What did you just say?"

Jesus speaks without moving his lips and it echoes in my head: *You clothed the naked, you aided the sick, you fed the starving, all these things you did for others, without care for harm that may befall you. There is no one greater than he who lays his life down for his friends.*

But I see myself with a pencil in my hand, poised over the church's ledger. Feeling that nausea every time I made a small erasure, changing an eight to a zero, that tiny niggling that told me *this is okay, you're only doing it one more time, but if you get caught, it's all over…*

I see myself writing those checks. For car payments. For vet's bills, for paying to shave a poor cat free of orange popsicle guck. For Tara's treatment. Always, always telling myself it was the last time, but then there would be a phone call, and an *I don't know what to do my cat will die if I don't get three hundred dollars from someplace,* and then I would offer, and the cycle would start over again…

I look at Jesus. He smiles.

We are plunged into dim orange light as

we enter the tunnel that takes our train through something called Space Mountain; our vehicle slows down and there is no more bumping, just a hum that vibrates my bones. My eyes adjust. Above us, a trinity of firing rocket engines and floating astronauts in space suits hover among shooting stars and glowing planets as silver bullet-shaped cars ascend lift hills. Below us, a diorama of a barren, reddish Mars-scape unfolds. Ethereal music, gleeful screaming, and the *clickety-clack* of the rollercoaster floods the tunnel.

You know what? I didn't take the stolen cash and squander it on fancy perfumes or gambling sprees. I didn't even buy toilet paper with that money. I gave it to everybody else. It's time to…let go. It's time to let myself off the hook and own up to everything.

And as luck would have it, I'm sharing a car with the best person to 'fess up to.

I make my way back into the booth and kneel before Jesus, who has one hand on each of his knees.

"You *bitch!*" Magda again. "You stay away from him!"

But the words pour forth. "Jesus, I am so sorry I stole money from my church and that's why I'm here, that's why I came here from Rhode Island and my real name isn't Livvie it's Samantha, and I am sorry, but I was doing it to help other people because I couldn't afford to help them alone and—"

He puts his warm hand on my head. "Greater is he that is in you than he that is in the world, man."

26

I'm about to continue, but Magda's made it to our booth and she's pulling my hair and shrieking like a Valkyrie. "He's *my* personal savior! He's *my* personal savior!"

Jesus tries to pull Magda off me.

The vehicle slams to a stop, and the lights inside the tunnel come on. Magda lets go of my hair, but my scalp is still throbbing. What had once been a sky full of stars is now just a painted black ceiling, and a steel rollercoaster rises in the center. The hanging planets I had seen before are, like…I dunno, huge pieces of paper hanging from wire. And a booming male voice tells space travelers to stay seated and the journey will continue shortly.

Six security guards stand at attention against the tunnel walls. "Would you come with us, please?"

"Oh, shit," Magda says.

Ejected, that's what happens next. *We're ejected from frigging Disney World.* They hustle us out of Tomorrowland and down the crowded Main Street where people are gazing at the fireworks in the sky with enlightened expressions. The guards have a firm but gentle grip on my arms and Magda begs like a widow in the throes of grief: "Please, please, we'll make certain it never happens again!"

They have Jesus bound at his wrists. They're pushing him, because he's not picking up his feet. "They know not what they're doing, man," he says, his voice full of sorrow. "Forgive them."

When we reach the transportation area on the shores of the lake, Jesus throws himself in the topiary garden and weeps.

Magda glares at me. "You *asshole.*"

But I couldn't care less if she's pissed off at me. I walk away in search of a cab.

It's Christmas Eve, and I have phone calls to make.

Charlotte's Family Tree

Charlotte noted the copy of *Swiss Family Robinson* on her daughter's night stand. "Is that the story Daddy read you tonight?"

Abby nodded. "Mommy, will you please take me to Disney World?"

And because Charlotte had never believed in telling her child half-truths or responding with vague answers, she said, "No."

* * *

Their New Year's Eve had carried an invulnerable air; Johnny had brought home three live lobsters, Charlotte had let herself get a little drunk, and they'd even let Abby stay up to watch the ball drop.

But after the question about Disney World, she wanted the night to end. She went into the master bedroom and stripped out of her velvet to get ready for bed—but through the sheer curtains, she could see the glow of a fire Johnny had going outside. She climbed into a sweatshirt and pulled up the hood; while she tied a loose knot under her chin, she noticed something on the dresser. Something she hadn't seen in a very long time, something she was sure was still buried in a trunk in the attic.

A framed photo of Charlotte and her Mom. Taken in 1979 in front of the Tropical Serenade in the Magic Kingdom. Charlotte was only eight, but two buds on her chest poked through her T-shirt;

next to her, her mother, who would have been forty that birthday had she lived, was all bones with a yellow tinge to her skin. The woman's orange halter top was stained, and even her wig looked like it had been dragged through a long ordeal.

She felt dizzy. "Johnny?" she called without thinking, but it came out a raspy squeak. And then she remembered he wasn't in the house.

She heard a *pop-clunk*—above her, in the attic. "Hello?"

No response.

With trembling fingers, she took the photo off the dresser, opened the top drawer, and buried it underneath her thigh-highs.

* * *

In the back yard, a light snow fell.

Still shaken, Charlotte stepped onto the brick patio and closed the slider behind her. Normally, she looked forward to the time she and Johnny had alone, but at that moment, she felt an unidentifiable weight between them.

"What now?" Johnny had wedged a snack-laden end table between the Adirondack chairs in front of their fire-pit—the bottom of an old Weber grill. He held a glass of champagne in each hand. "We had a nice night, it doesn't have to be over yet. What's wrong? She didn't go down okay or what?"

She hesitated, knowing that if she went further, it might garner one of his occasional 'quit-being-a-sad-sack' lectures, and she wasn't in the mood. "Everything's fine," she said. She glanced over at the bedroom window and half-expected to see someone peer back at her.

Johnny looked in that direction, too. "What?"

"Nothing. I'm just tired." She nodded to the spread he'd put out. "A lot of food. Dinner wasn't enough?"

He shrugged. "Hey, it's not New Year's without the damn cheese ball. At least not in my estimation. Happy New Year." He kissed her on the cheek, handed her a glass of champagne, and sat down in a chair. "Cheers."

She raised her glass and forced a smile. "Cheers."

He guzzled what was in his glass, set it down on the table, and reached for a cracker. "So, everything is fine."

Charlotte nodded. "Yeah."

"Hey, she loved that lobster. Just next time we should remember to maybe take that roe out of there. It was nasty." He cut into the cheese ball and balanced a hard pink bit of it on a Wheat Thin. "Funny thing is it only seemed to bother me." He chuckled. "I can't believe she ate it."

"It's the same stuff that's in the Chinese egg rolls," Charlotte answered.

"She's growing up fast," he said. "A little too fast, if you ask me. You know she wants to go to the pond to look for chickadees tomorrow by herself?"

"Did you tell her she could?"

"Why not?" He bit into the cracker. "It's just on the back of the property and she already waits at the bus stop by herself, she goes to the library by herself. What's the difference?"

A snowflake landed on Charlotte's eyelid; she let it melt. The fire was going enough so that her shins, even through her sweatpants, were getting hot.

"Which brings me to the next thing I wanted to mention at dinner tonight, but thought I should wait until now." He put another lump of cheese on a cracker and offered it to her, but she shook her head. He shrugged and put it in his mouth. "I did a lot of research today online and I'm thinking we should take Abby to Disney World. Like in the next week or so."

Charlotte shivered, but not because a gust had rushed in from somewhere, and not because a few snowflakes pelted her cheek.

She hadn't realized until that moment that this conversation had always been inevitable. From the day she'd discovered she was pregnant it had been looming in the back of her mind, because a trip to Disney World, in her family *and* in Johnny's, was a rite of passage. Their parents had taken *them*, and it was expected that when they had children they would take *theirs*, and not doing it was just shirking some kind of parental responsibility. A third of her was relieved. A third of her was terrified.

And the other third of her had just figured out that the dinner, the book, and the photo had all been part of a plan.

Johnny didn't notice. "We can get out of this crappy weather, and the rates down there are cheaper because it's not that busy between New Year's and Martin Luther King Day weekend. The college doesn't open until the end of January anyway, and I've got no problem pulling her out of school. She's way ahead of everybody in her class." He stabbed at a log with a fireplace poker. Sparks burst skyward. "She's going to be seven in February. I think we should take her. Most of her friends have been there, and it's not that I want to keep up with the Jones' or anything, but she's really the right age."

Charlotte was seething, but wasn't quite sure how to articulate everything she felt at the moment: Had Abby been a willing participant in this? Did Johnny *actually* think these tricks were going to sway her?

Johnny rested the poker against the side of the house and wiped his hands on his jeans. "So what do you think?"

She looked over at him, and all that came out was "That was a shitty thing to do, Johnny."

"Excuse me?"

"The dinner was fine, the book was obvious but the photo was just going too far."

"Whoa." He put his hands on his hips. "What are you talking about?"

Charlotte rose from her chair. "You read her *Swiss Family Robinson* and told her there was a treehouse there? She asked me tonight if we could please take her to Disney. And the book was next to the bed. And one of those horrible photos of my Mom that's been up in the trunk and hasn't seen the light of day in years was on my dresser. *That's* really unfair."

Johnny was quiet. Then he let out an exasperated sigh, and she knew what that meant. "The fact that I decided to read her *Swiss Family Robinson* had nothing to do with the Disney business. She wanted to know who Johann David Wyss was because she saw the award in my office. You're paranoid."

"But you *did* mention it, didn't you?"

"Look, yes, I mentioned it. And as far as the damn photo's concerned, there's no lock on that attic door. She probably got it herself." He sat back down in his chair, stared into the fire, and muttered, "I should hope you'd know me better than that."

There was only the sound of the wind.

Finally, Johnny spoke. "She's a *kid*, alright? Now I know you're not a big fan of Disney World and all of that, and I know you had a big traumatic experience down there in the Treehouse. But her childhood isn't anything like yours was, and I think sometimes, angel, you…go a little overboard." He sat back down and poured more champagne in each of their glasses. "She's going to go down there, and she'll have a *good* experience. Pretty soon we're going to have our hands full with her thinking about boys and eye shadow, and I don't want you sitting there feeling guilty when she's thirty and she's coming back to you asking you why we never took her to Disney

World. Here." He handed her the refilled champagne glass.

She blinked and looked at him.

"At the rate she's going, Charlotte, she's going to be too big and miss all the magic." He reached for her hand, and squeezed it, hard, like he did when he delivered bad news. "I'll call tomorrow and make reservations, and I swear, you won't have to go anywhere near that Treehouse, okay? I'll handle that."

A burning log popped, and the snow fell harder.

* * *

The trip on which the incident had happened had been spontaneous, too. Not because Charlotte and her younger twin brothers had been in danger of being too old, but because their mother had been in danger of dying.

On their first day her father told her that Disney World was the most magical place on earth. By ten that morning, though, Charlotte disagreed: nothing had changed. Being in Disney World hadn't magically spared her of being responsible for the twins. Being in Disney World hadn't magically made her Mom better…the violent cough hadn't magically stopped the moment they'd set foot on Main Street.

Charlotte hadn't even been allowed to carry her own ticket book: "We need to stick together as a family, because I need you to help me with your Mom and the twins," her Dad had said. "Besides, you don't want to lose the tickets."

But Charlotte knew she wouldn't lose them. She was old enough to carry her own money; old enough to pack the twins' lunches; old enough to mete out her mother's pills when Dad was at work. She was old enough to dust the living room, clean the toilets, and put the twins' laundry in the washing machine. In her estimation, she should have been allowed to not only have her own book of tickets, but go anywhere in Disney World—*at least* in Disney World!—by herself.

So as a family, they had gone on If You Had Wings and Mission to Mars, and Charlotte had hoped she'd go up so high she'd never come back down; they had ridden Mr. Toad's Wild Ride and she'd hoped when their car had emerged they'd be in some other world; at the end of 20,000 Leagues Under the Sea she'd been disappointed to discover they hadn't arrived in Atlantis. And when each fantasy ended, they were back out in the sunny plazas looking for the nearest bench so they could let Mom *rest*.

And just when Charlotte had been certain that the whole concept of 'the most magical place on earth' was nothing more than the most violating kind of lie a parent could ever tell a child, one of their rest periods landed them in a shaded area across from the Swiss Family Treehouse.

She had always wanted a real treehouse in the yard; she had asked her father, but he had said, "it's not a good idea, sweetheart. With the twins and your Mom being so sick, I really need you to be close by at all times. If there's an emergency, or I need you to do something in a hurry, I can't be climbing trees looking for you." She had prayed for God to grow a treehouse in her yard; she had even wished for a treehouse on the evening star. And all of that had proven futile. Until that moment, in Adventureland, where her treehouse—and not just any treehouse, the MOTHER-OF-ALL-TREEHOUSES—called to her with its scent of indoor swimming pools and jasmine and the sounds of festive organ music. The Swiss Family Treehouse was the place she'd been looking for, the place where no one could reach her.

All she needed was a B Ticket.

"I'm going to get us some pineapple juices," her father said. "You all stay here until I get back."

"Can I go in the Treehouse now?" Charlotte asked.

"When I get back. You be a good girl and entertain the twins."

Charlotte envied the other kids skipping by her. They didn't know how good they had it.

The twins whined and clambered all over her mother, who was coughing while she tried to control them.

"Charlotte," her mother tried to make her voice forceful. "Take these kids, will you?"

But Charlotte was dreaming about the Treehouse.

"Charlotte Ann. Help me like you're supposed to."

Just then, her mother's quilted bag fell off the bench and spilled its innards, and a strange impulse came over Charlotte. In a move so swift she shocked even herself, she swiped one of the ticket books and ran.

"Charlotte!" she heard her mother gasp.

Charlotte had never been very good in gym class; she was chubby and her ankles hurt when she ran. But that day, she didn't feel the pain; she felt instead like she had wings on her feet.

She gave the woman her ticket and the tree embraced her. A giant wheel spun and bamboo cups ferried water from a running stream to the upper levels; stairs upon stairs snaked through the boughs; there was a bedroom with a skylight where at night she could look out at the stars; there was a sink fashioned from a giant clam shell and an organ that played by itself; and there was, at last, her little bedroom. With three hammocks and a desk and a bureau.

"Charlotte!" *Thunk, thunk, thunk.* "You get back here!"

Mom was coming up the stairs.

No, no, no, she was not going back down there. She was going to live in the Treehouse. She was going to sleep in one of the little hammocks and smell oranges and coconuts for the rest of her life. There was a door to the little room and she tried to pull it open, but it was locked tight. She got down on her knees and tried to crawl underneath it, but she was too fat.

Her mother appeared at the base of the narrow stairs. "Charlotte," she gasped, and reached for her as she limped up one stair at a time. There was only one way for Charlotte to go, and that was down.

The way Mom was coming up.

Suddenly her mother stopped, clutched the

handrail, collapsed, and fell down the stairs.

A week later, Charlotte's mother was dead.

* * *

The Boardwalk Inn's arched entranceway gaped like a huge mouth. They got off the Magical Express bus, and Johnny stood with his hands on his hips, surveying land he'd just conquered; she was half-surprised he didn't have one hand tucked into his jacket.

"This place is nice, right?" He set his hand on her lower back. Abby ran ahead to the white cottage-style front doors.

"It's very nice," she responded with feigned interest.

But when they stepped inside, she was pleased. The place *was* carousel beautiful; white and gold and clean and bright with polished hardwood floors, gilded lamps, mahogany tables, flower-patterned settees and palm trees in the corners.

"Look at that!" Abby pointed to a chandelier. Golden horses with mermaid tails merry-go-rounded its center.

It was the opposite of the dark hole they'd stayed in during *that* trip; Charlotte remembered devilish Tiki gods lurking in every corner and a cavernous room full of screeching tropical birds. Here, nothing leered at her; here, the only noise was the pleasant sound of a band playing a Charleston.

"I'll go check us in," Johnny said.

She watched Abby put her arms out and twirl,

her ice blue dress billowing. Charlotte's mother had made her a dress like that when she was younger than Abby; she had dubbed it her Alice in Wonderland dress and worn it until the seams split. She'd asked her mother to sew it back together for her, and had left it on the sewing table.

She'd always hoped it would show up, repaired, next to her birthday cake or under the Christmas tree, but it never had.

She noticed Abby was talking to herself.

"No, she bought this for me at the big mall," Abby said.

Out of the corner of her eye, she caught Johnny waving her over to the front desk. "I'll be right there," she mouthed. She turned back to Abby. "Honey, I'll be right—"

But Abby was gone.

"Abby?" she called, scanning the room. But she didn't see her—or any other children, either. "Abby!"

A door easing shut attracted her attention. Outside? *Had she gone outside?*

"Abby!" She ran through the doors, down a long flight of steps, and into the pool area, seized by a panic she didn't quite understand. She caught the flutter of light blue fabric through the trees. "Abby!"

She stopped when she saw what was ahead of her: a giant clown with a roller coaster structure behind it—the pool's water slide.

Abby was at the top, ready to slide down.

"Get down from there!"

But Abby sat down and all Charlotte saw was the top of her head, whizzing around a corner and out of sight. She splashed into the pool, shoes and all.

"Abby, *damn* you!"

Four or five people turned and stared at her, and behind her, she heard Johnny laugh.

"We had your swimsuit in my backpack, you know!" he shouted.

"I'm glad you think this is funny," Charlotte said. "She just ran off!"

He frowned. "She goes in the pool all the time at home by herself. She's a good swimmer and there's a lifeguard right there."

"That's not the point. She *ran off*."

Abby climbed up out of the pool and spattered her way over to them. Her dress clung to her legs.

Charlotte seized her daughter's wrist. "That was not funny, young lady. We ought to put you back on that plane right now and take your ass home."

"Hey." Johnny grabbed Charlotte's arm. "What is *with* you?"

"She had better not pull this shit again while we're here, Johnny, I mean it."

"Stop it," he murmured, glancing over at the occupied patio chairs by the hot tub. "People are staring."

Abby burst into tears.

He shot Charlotte an angry look, then turned his attention to Abby. "Your Mom's just not feeling well right now, honey." He set down his backpack, unzipped it, and pulled out a small pink bag. "Here's your bathing suit, now why don't you go to that building over there and get changed, okay? And when you come back, you can go down the slide a few times if you want, so no more tears."

Abby threw her arms around Johnny's neck, but never took her hurt, angry gaze off Charlotte.

Charlotte shuddered.

She watched Abby walk away. The girl's shoulders were hunched, and her sopping wet dress left a trail of water drips on the cement. Charlotte saw the people by the hot tub and knew that they were only pretending to read their magazines; she knew that behind their sunglasses, their eyes were on her defeated daughter. And she felt guilty, because she recognized the scene. What *had* she been she so upset about? "I don't want to make her hate me," she said. "I'm sorry. I don't know what I was thinking."

Johnny nodded in the direction of the bar, a red-striped structure shaped like a circus tent with LEAPING HORSE LIBATIONS lettered on bright yellow banners. "Why don't we just go have a drink," he said.

They climbed up on neighboring barstools and Johnny reached for his wallet. "Yelling in Disney World. You're something else, you know that? Abby's been here ten minutes and all she's doing is wondering why the hell you're limiting her and screaming at her on top of it. She wasn't doing anything we don't let her do at home."

"She took off," Charlotte said.

He raised an eyebrow. "She does at home."

"She *tells* us where she's going."

He raised his other eyebrow.

She relented. "Okay, maybe I shouldn't have yelled, but I got really frightened."

The bartender lifted the stack of paper coasters emblazoned with DISNEY'S BOARDWALK and wiped the counter underneath them.

"Give me a Johnny Walker Black straight up and a glass of red wine for her," Johnny said. "Please."

The bartender nodded and went to the other end of the bar; Charlotte thought he was going to turn back to her to say something, but then changed his mind.

Johnny set a hand on top of hers. "Look, this trip got off to a bad start and we should start over. But let me tell you something. You ruin this for her and you'll be the one I'm putting on a plane. Because I've just had enough. You've sulked from day one and I'm done."

The bartender set their drinks in front of them.

"We're going to the Magic Kingdom tomorrow. If you don't want to come, you don't have to. But you're going to be missing out." He picked up his glass. "Now, cheers."

Charlotte clinked glasses with him and tried to dispel the dread.

* * *

Surprisingly, there had been frost the night before, and a chilly breeze whipped off the lake as they approached the Magic Kingdom's Main Gate; Charlotte, however, was sweating. Abby skipped a few yards ahead of them and occasionally stopped to dance to music pumping from inside the park; Charlotte thought she recognized a tune from *The Music Man*.

"Abby, don't go so far!" she called.

"She's fine," Johnny said. "Let her do her thing. Hey, check these out." He pointed at the walk in front of them, which was tiled with octagonal bricks. They were etched with messages: WE LOVE YOU GRANDMA! THE SMITH CHILDREN and WE MISS YOU LULU 1946-1986. Each brick also had the familiar Mickey Mouse symbol.

They reminded Charlotte of grave markers.

She reached out and gripped Johnny's arm. "I can't…I can't do this."

He looked back at her. "Yes, you can." He nodded in Abby's direction. "Look at how happy she is."

Charlotte eyed Abby, who had already reached the row of admission gates and was jumping up and down, waving at them to hurry up.

"I guess…I guess we can let her carry her own ticket book," Charlotte said.

Johnny laughed. "Honey, there are no more ticket books, there haven't been for a lot of years now. It's all single admission and our hotel keys get us in." He dug into his back pocket and retrieved his wallet to pull out his key and Abby's. "You brought yours?"

Charlotte nodded, and a weight lifted from

her as her card was sucked through the slot and she slipped through the turnstile.

"See?" Johnny said, shoving his wallet back in his pocket, "You set foot in the Magic Kingdom and nothing bad happened."

Yet, Charlotte thought. Johnny handed her a park map, and she opened it with trembling fingers, expecting to see If You Had Wings, Mission to Mars, Mr. Toad's Wild Ride and 20,000 Leagues Under the Sea. Perhaps there was a way they could just avoid all those rides; she was certain there had to be plenty of other things to do. But when she looked at the listing of attractions, she was surprised to find that none of what she'd remembered was on the list.

"They closed them," she said aloud, although she hadn't meant to.

"Closed what?" Johnny asked.

"Oh…just…some things I remembered."

"It was a long time ago, I told you. Things are different."

She looked again at the map, specifically at Adventureland, hoping the Treehouse was gone, too.

It wasn't. It was still there.

He gripped her hand, and she caught sight of Abby, skipping down the street, admiring everything around her. She had a sudden flashback of that day, then: the kids that had passed her as she sat on that miserable bench. How envious she'd been of them, that they had freedom. That they were allowed to be kids.

She needed to just let Abby, she decided, be a kid. And though she kept careful watch, as they went from Tomorrowland to the Tea Cups and Small World to Splash Mountain, she caught herself not only enjoying, but reveling in Abby's fun. Abby tromped around in the Sleeping Beauty dress they'd bought her, and when she posed for a photo with The Little Mermaid, she said that someday she'd live under the sea, too. Charlotte regretted having kept her daughter's life as Disney-free as possible. While Johnny and Abby were at The Country Bears Jamboree, she stole away to the gift shop so she could get the girl a few things for her birthday.

As she filled up a bag of fake jewels at a shop called Tinker Bell's Treasures, she thought, *this is a new Disney World. This place does have magic.*

But her euphoria only lasted until just before sunset, when they entered a breezeway and heard the drums that signaled their impending arrival in Adventureland. She pulled on Johnny's hand. "Maybe we should go. It *is* getting late, and we have dinner reservations in two hours."

"We can hit a couple of things in here now, we've got time."

But she didn't take another step. "I…wanted to clean up a little bit, get Abby out of that dress and into something different—"

Johnny faced her and set a hand on her shoulder; he reached up and brushed a strand of hair away from her face. "This has been a great day and you've done great. Abby's having a blast and so are we, right? Let's not go wrecking it."

She looked deeper into the crowded breezeway. People filled the benches outside the restrooms, clogged the entrance to a tropical-themed gift shop, and huddled around their double-strollers and massive backpacks. But there still weren't enough of them to completely obstruct the view of what was beyond.

The base of the Treehouse.

Abby rushed ahead of them. Johnny and Charlotte found her out in the plaza, pointing to the tree's boughs. "She's up there today."

Johnny crouched down. "No, Cinderella lives in the castle. The Swiss Family Robinson lives up there, like I told you," he said.

"Let's go *now*!" Abby clapped her hands and handed Charlotte the light-up Tinker Bell wand. "Can you hold this, Mommy?"

Charlotte wasn't listening. She remembered the defiance, the anger, the lawlessness of the moment she'd swiped that ticket book; she remembered feeling hopelessly trapped with nowhere to go but to her ailing mother; she saw her mother fall and heard her chip-thin thighs crack on the way down. It hit her that her daughter was just a year younger than Charlotte had been on that day.

She grabbed her husband's arm. "Please don't take her up there."

He stood up. "It's all going to be fine, angel."

"Let's go, Daddy!"

"In a minute, Abbs. Just hang on one second,

will you?" He lowered his voice. "Why don't you go over to the Bazaar and look at some dresses or whatever—see if you'd maybe like something new to wear to dinner tonight. I'll take her, and when we come down, we'll go do Pirates or something and then maybe we'll have time to do one more thing before we've gotta head back to the hotel."

Charlotte hesitated. She looked up at the Treehouse, its leaves aflutter in the breeze; she looked at Abby, who was fidgeting in anticipation; she looked at Johnny's earnest expression, and it struck her that he had been enormously patient. More than patient. And if she let them go up in the Treehouse, just this once, they would never want to do it again. They would move on with their vacation and visit the other parks, visit the places that weren't even in existence in 1979. Charlotte would go home with her daughter, her husband, and enough happy memories that her very first trip would feel like it had never happened, and she'd feel silly she'd even put up such a stink. "Fine," she said, and watched them walk, hand in hand, up to the sign that read SWISS FAMILY TREEHOUSE.

* * *

When Charlotte came out of the gift shop, her husband sat alone. "Where's Abby?"

"I thought you were going to be awhile yet." He shifted on the bench to make room for her. "Did you get nice stuff?"

"*Where is she?*"

He didn't answer, and she recognized his

hand-in-the-cookie jar look.

"You let her go back up there by *herself*?"

"*It's Disney World and nothing's going to happen.*" He stood up. "Be reasonable, I'm right here. I'm sure she's fine. She really wanted to go again and take another look at the organ room up there and I just couldn't climb any more stairs."

But Charlotte was furious, and without another thought, she went off toward the Treehouse.

"Charlotte!" He yelled after her. "She's going to come back here! I can't come with you!"

But she ignored him and went up to the Treehouse entrance, prepared to march right up the stairs.

Until she set her foot across the threshold. Something about the fake wood under her feet, something about the smell, indoor swimming pool and jasmine, brought her back. She felt the clothes she wore that day, her little blue jean skort and Alice in Wonderland T-shirt, her Mickey Mouse ears with her name embroidered on them. She could feel sweat in her hair, because the ears were a heavy material and they were hot.

"Ma'am," said a Cast Member, HARVEY. "It's a little past dusk so we're going to be closing this down."

She couldn't turn back. "My daughter," she said. "My daughter is up there."

HARVEY eyed her. "I haven't seen a little girl in awhile, Ma'am. Are you sure?"

Charlotte ran. She ran across the suspension bridge. She grabbed the hand rails and wished she could take the stairs two at a time, but they weren't the normal rise, she remembered that, and taking them that way would trip her up.

"Abby!" she screamed. "Abby, it's Mommy!"

No answer. She raced past the library, nearly stumbling as she grabbed hold of the newel post at the base of another flight of stairs. The music had gone from a bass *thump-thump-thump* to a real melody as she got closer.

Above her, she heard her daughter's giggle, and voices. "Abby!"

But when she reached the organ room with its giant clam shell sink and dining room table set with china, her daughter wasn't there and the music had stopped.

Then she saw the flash of the girl's princess gown, on the other side of the organ room. "Why thank you for that dance!" Abby said.

Charlotte rounded the corner, seized her daughter, picked her up, held her close. She wanted to yell at Abby for scaring her, but the girl's smell, cotton candy and tulle, calmed her. This was real. Abby was real. She was okay, and Charlotte was going to make damn sure the both of them got out of the Treehouse in one piece. "I'm so glad you're okay."

"It's okay, Mommy, I had fun. A lady let me go into that room and we danced to the music. She told me only special kids get to do that. It was good."

Charlotte looked at the doors that were locked and latched to keep guests from walking into the displays; then, she took a deep breath and laughed.

A Cast Member had been with Abby the whole time. "Come on, sweetie." She set her daughter down. "Let's go find Daddy and get ready for dinner."

"But I want to say goodbye to the lady," Abby said.

"I'm sure the lady's busy making sure the Treehouse is all shut down." Charlotte took her hand, and the two of them made their way down the stairs, past the kitchen with its fake fruit and back over the jouncing suspended bridge.

When they got to the bottom, HARVEY stretched a rope with a sign that said CLOSED across the Treehouse entrance.

* * *

On George Washington's Birthday weekend, a blizzard dumped two feet of snow. Charlotte busied herself in the kitchen making lamb stew while Johnny was out shoveling the walk; she sat peeling carrots at the table. In the living room, she could hear Abby, who sat in front of the fireplace while she painted in a Cinderella coloring book Charlotte had bought in Disney World. Abby was talking to herself, but the conversation Charlotte heard was not the usual conversation with imaginary friends, all "the ship is sinking! We have to jump onto the raft!" or "Ernst, I think you should let your brother ride the ostrich."

Instead, she heard Abby say, "Well, I'm very sorry about that. Mommy doesn't always see things the way she should. Even Daddy says that sometimes."

Charlotte set aside the carrot and put down

the peeler. "Abby?"

A momentary silence, then, "Yeah?"

"What game are you playing now, sweetheart?"

"I'm talking to the lady."

Charlotte frowned and got up. She grabbed the kitchen towel next to the microwave, wiped her hands, and leaned against the wall that separated the kitchen and the living room. "What lady?"

"She says she used to be a princess."

Charlotte, satisfied, turned back into the kitchen, broke a carrot stick in half, and popped it into her mouth.

"You know her, Mommy. We have a picture of her."

Charlotte nearly choked. "What?"

"You have a picture of her."

She closed her eyes and managed to swallow the carrot despite a knot in her esophagus—and then she nearly laughed at herself when she realized it was probably a picture of the lady who'd let Abby dance in the organ room at the Treehouse—Johnny had probably taken it.

"You mean in the Disney trip album?"

"No, over the fireplace."

Charlotte had to admit she rarely looked at what was over the fireplace; she paid a woman to come and clean. Still, she was familiar with the photos on the mantle: she and Johnny climbing out of the limousine at their wedding; Abby when she was a toddler, sitting in a laundry basket with bananas all over her face; a double frame with Charlotte receiving her Master's degree on one side and Johnny winning the Johann David Wyss Award on the other; Johnny and his brothers at a baseball game. She searched among them, expecting to spy a photo of Abby and Johnny in the Swiss Family Treehouse.

But when she looked she saw there wasn't one. There was, instead, a black and white photo of a woman in a long, white gown with a tiara on her head and a ribbon across her bodice that read "Miss Connecticut 1964."

It was her mother. Another photo that had been locked away in the attic for years.

Charlotte looked at Abby, who was daubing red paint on Cinderella's gown. She remembered what Johnny had said about the mysterious appearance of the picture on her dresser: *Abby probably got it herself.* Furious, she seized her daughter's wrists. The paintbrush went flying. "I want you to stay out of that that attic, do you hear me?" she screamed. "If I ever *catch* you up there, if I ever catch you *playing* with *anything* you got from up there, I will punish you like you have *never* been punished before!"

"But I didn't do it!" Abby burst into tears. "I didn't do it! The lady gave them to me!"

"You stop it! Stop it, stop it, stop lying!"

The bottle of red paint tipped over, and a puddle crept across the floor.

"I'm not!" Abby struggled to get free of Charlotte's grip. "You didn't listen to her and she's real mad at you! She says she's never going to leave you alone! And I *hate* you!"

Charlotte felt like she was going to throw up, but she only gripped Abby tighter. Abby's wailing filled the room, and each shriek felt like it was piercing Charlotte's lung.

Johnny burst through the front door in a torrent of snow. "What the *hell* is going on in here?"

But Charlotte couldn't answer, and Abby finally squirmed free of her mother's grasp and ran to Johnny's arms.

Romancing the Goat

I shouldn't have done what I did, but it wasn't because she was albino—I felt bad for her albino-ness or whatever you call it; I had a crossed eye growing up, and until it was fixed, people picked on me because I looked like a freak. So that wasn't why I did it, I swear.

I did it because Angelina was meaner than a tipped cow from the day Mom and Dad rescued her from a foster home.

That first night, she was camped out with her five dilapidated boxes in the freshly-painted butter yellow room across from mine. I was nervous. *Be extra sensitive Imogene*, Mom had said, *both of her parents are dead.* So I hesitated in front of her door. That's when I heard it.

She was talking to someone. Or something: "Of course not. This time it will be much easier," she was saying.

"Angelina." I knocked.

The murmuring stopped. Silence.

"Come on," I said. "I just…I just wanna say hi."

I heard footfalls and then the door opened, only enough for her narrow face to block my view of the room beyond. Her hair was white as flour, and her eyes were pink. "What." The word came out like a bee sting.

"I just…I'm…your new sister. Immy."

She blinked. "Hello," she said, with church

picnic politeness.

"I'm…sorry about your Mom and Dad—"

She snorted. "They did something stupid." She started to close her door.

"Wait." I stopped her. I elevated myself on my toes to try and peer over her head, but all I could see was the open window, the flood-lit orange tree in the front yard. "Who were you talking to? You could always talk to me if—"

"None of your business."

She closed the door.

* * *

The next day at breakfast, Angelina dumped half the bottle of syrup on her empty plate, guzzled down a glass of orange juice, refilled it, and then guzzled that. She dipped her hand in the syrup and licked the runny stuff from her fingers.

"Angelina, honey, you don't have to eat *just* the syrup." Mom buttoned up her suit jacket; she was showing a house that day. "We may be an all-organic household but we have plenty. You can have all you want here." She kissed her on the top of her head.

Skeins of syrup ran down Angelina's left arm.

"Guess what," I said. "Aurora says I'm good enough to be head cheerleader next year."

No one responded. Mom was smiling at Angelina in a way that I'd only seen on Christmas card Virgin Marys. Dad was humming "You are my Sunshine" as he flipped the pancakes.

I was as insignificant as a fly stuck between windowpanes.

"Um, Mom? Dad?" I cleared my throat. "I need to eat first because Aurora's coming to pick me up because we have cheerleading practice before school."

"Oh, Immy, you don't have to raise your voice," Mom said. "And anyway, it's Angelina's first breakfast here, so she gets first batch. In fact, we even got her something extra special to celebrate." Mom slipped her hand in her pocket and extracted a small gold box with a blue ribbon.

Angelina blinked—in surprise, but there was something feigned about it—at Mom. Then, with her sticky, drippy hands, she opened the box, rummaged through the tissue paper, and pulled out a silver charm bracelet.

Exactly the one they'd bought me for my sixteenth birthday.

I saw red. "That's mine!"

"No, it's not, dear." Mom twittered and took the bracelet from Angelina to open the clasp and put it on her wrist. "It's just the same one as yours, since you liked yours so much. You know what they say, it's just like real estate. If it's successful once, don't mess with the formula."

Angelina's weird pink eyes met mine.

"But she didn't do anything to deserve that." I looked at Dad, but I was getting no support there. "She hasn't even been to school yet and she's only gonna be a freshman."

Dad set three pancakes on Angelina's plate, and she gobbled so recklessly it made me think of the pigs in the races I'd seen at the fair. When I thought that, I guffawed so loud I shocked even myself. "And she'll get it all dirty. Look at her! She doesn't even use a fork!"

Angelina burst into tears, ran to her room, and slammed the door.

"Imogene Marie! Really!" Mom went after her.

I scrambled to think if I should defend myself. The only sound in the kitchen was butter sizzling.

Dad stood there, his brow furrowed. "Immy," he said. "This is important to your mother, so do what she says and please let's keep the peace, okay?"

He peered quickly down the hall in the direction Mom had gone, then he came over and slid two pancakes onto my plate. By the time I put butter on them, they were cold.

* * *

Over the next few weeks, I learned to tolerate Angelina at the table and tried to be civil, but she had no interest in talking to me. And there was seriously something *wrong* with this girl. Every time I cruised by her room, I heard weird stuff. Low murmurs, Something like the *Aum* on Mom's ridiculous *Yoga for Youga!* DVD. Snorts and grunts. And words I couldn't make out.

I frequently pressed my ear to her door.

"We're going to have everything we wanted.

Not like before," she said once to whoever she was talking to.

And then she started *doing* things to get me in trouble. I came home after cheerleading practice and my dirty panties confettied the hall. Chocolate was forbidden in our house, but somehow Angelina found ways to bring it in and melt it into the furniture. Then she'd stick the wrapper near my stuff, or in my room, so Mom would find it. She tore the covers off Dad's *True West* magazines, melted the rubber top to Mom's juicer, and took a permanent marker and wrote "smelly" on her own bedroom door.

"What is going on with you, Immy? Are you acting out?" Mom sat at the small desk in her office, her suit jacket draped over the back of the chair, her hands folded on her lap. "The psychologists all say that the non-adopted sibling has problems adjusting, and that certain…issues may arise, but this is a little extreme. I thought you always said you didn't want to be an only child."

"Actually…" I didn't know where she'd gotten that from. I had never said that. "Mom, she…" I heard footsteps coming down the hall, but they stopped by the door, as though someone was listening. I dropped my voice to a whisper. "She's *weird*. She talks to herself—or *something*—every night in her room. It's creepy."

"Stop that, now. We need to give her space. She's adjusting."

"She dumped out my laundry and melted your juicer," I said.

"Immy. Be reasonable."

"Why don't you believe me? Have I ever lied to you?"

Mom sighed, that same sigh she did when she saw Dad drink a diet soda. "No, Immy, you haven't. But your actions that first day at the breakfast table set the tone, so what am I supposed to think? I'm sure she wouldn't destroy property. Her foster family just said she was a little…erratic, but consider what she's been through. Stop trying so hard to get attention. *I* know you're here." Her cell phone rang, but she didn't reach for it right away. Instead, she said, "I understand, honey. I really do. But I expect more from you. Until she gets more settled, you're going to have to get used to being second fiddle for a little bit." She flipped open her phone. "Consuela Barnes…why, yes, that house is still available…"

I turned to leave.

"…hold on one minute…Immy? Would you mind running to Bountiful's and getting me some more of those organic carrots? You know the ones?"

* * *

"This just sucks," I said to Aurora as I shimmied out of my jeans. We were skipping seventh period Botany in favor of a dip in the lake. "I'm getting blamed for this juvenile shit."

Aurora was untying her halter top. "I can't believe your 'rents don't notice this chick is a complete freako." She gathered her long red hair and put it up with a scrunchy.

"Mom says it's because her parents are dead. That's her rationale."

"Oh my God, my hair's full of knots. Did you bring a hairbrush?"

"Yeah." I reached into my book bag, which didn't hold anything *except* the brush, a change of clothes, and a Twinkie I was going to have to eat before I got home so Mom wouldn't catch me.

"Well, I could see that, I guess." Aurora bent over and ran my brush through her hair. "With how they died, and all."

I realized I didn't know how they'd died. "How?"

"Your parents don't know? Jeez, you don't know? I thought everybody did. It was all over the school like a couple of weeks ago." She tossed me back my brush and ran straight into the water, diving head-first.

I followed and stroked out to just beyond where my feet could touch.

Aurora treaded water next to me. "Jimmy? His sister Jewels' best friend Sybil is in Mr. Botts' freshman Home-Ec with Angelina. Some dumb bitch burned a hole in a double-boiler 'cuz she didn't know to put water in it, and Angelina started freakin' out when she saw all the smoke on the gas stove and told Mr. Botts her parents died in a big barn explosion, so now Angelina doesn't have to take Home-Ec anymore because being around the flame is too traumatizing." Aurora floated on her back.

I thought of some of the things I'd heard

through her closed door: *we'll always have what we want, now. We'll do whatever we have to do.* "Oh, please," I said. "Angelina's a lying sack of shit."

"I don't think so. Jimmy's brother's babysitter's Dad works for the fire department. There *was* a big barn fire a couple months back. It's probably true, and you heard it here first! Come on. Race ya to the dock." And then she stretched out her arms and headed for a bunch of logs we'd had some guys on the football team lash together and anchor to a sunken Pinto far below.

But I didn't follow her right away, because what she'd said was niggling at me. What if it were true? What if it were true and Angelina *saw it*? Saw the whole thing? Or worse, saw the whole thing and then their charred-up bodies? That was a terrible way for her parents to go. For the first time since Angelina's initial night in our house, I found myself feeling bad for the girl.

Until Aurora climbed onto the raft and her bracelet gleamed in the sun, and it reminded me of the one I got for my sixteenth birthday, the same one Mom and Dad bought for Angelina.

* * *

That night, Mom and Dad were out at their Grateful Grainlovers meeting and I was feeling bold enough to ask Angelina to her face how her parents had died. But just before I was about to reach for the knob, I heard her laugh. "Wait until you see!"

And something, something in that room...

something talked back. A long, low groan.

It spooked me enough to wish Mom and Dad were home. I was alone in the house with Angelina and…and *something else*.

And then the door flew open and I jumped several feet. She glared at me. "What."

Like on the first night, I tried to peer inside her room, but to no avail. "I just…" I had been planning to blurt, *I just wanted to ask you how your parents died,* but she'd startled the crap out of me, and all I could stammer was, "…who…who are you…talking to?"

She sneered. "I am reading aloud. I like to read aloud. And you quit listening at my door, or else."

She went to slam the door on me, but that's when I saw it: she had not just the charm bracelet on that Mom and Dad had given her, *but mine too*. I stuck my ankle into the door so she couldn't close it and grabbed her wrist. "That's my bracelet!"

For one second I thought I saw a glimmer of surprise, but then she said with an indignant little toss of her head, "I want it."

"You can't have it. You got your own. Give it back."

"No."

From the room behind her I heard a low rumble.

"Give. It. Back!" I shoved the door with so much force it opened all the way and banged against the wall.

Holy hell.

Her room was crammed with goats. Stuffed goats—white, black, brown, wearing tutus. Porcelain goats of all sizes. Her bedspread was a goat pattern and her throw pillow was a goat. In the corner, her cardboard boxes served as pedestals for burning candles in the shapes of goats. And it looked like she had taken crayons and drawn goats on the fresh paint-job. "What the—"

Just then, Mom and Dad walked through the front door, and Angelina started hyperventilating and whipped up a whole barrel-full of fake tears.

"What is going *on* in here?" Mom rushed in.

"She took my bracelet!"

"Imogene Marie, she has her own. *Why* would she do that?"

"But look—" I raised my hand to point at the sobbing Angelina as proof, but when I did, I saw that *both bracelets were somehow on my wrist.*

Mom looked like a wounded calf. "Please," she said quietly. "Just go to your room."

* * *

It was shortly after that Mom and Dad decided the best way to improve things was to take us to Disneyland. We only lived a couple of hours away, and I'd been several times. Angelina had never been. So they thought that by forcing me to take her on her first attractions, I'd somehow develop more sisterly behavior patterns.

"I don't like anything fast, and I don't like anything that's in the dark, and I don't like loud noises," Angelina said.

I was about to develop more sisterly behavior patterns, alright. I smiled, reached out and took Angelina's hand. Mom beamed.

"I know this great ride that has goats on it," I said.

Angelina blinked, and for the first time since I'd known her, she smiled—genuinely. "Really?"

"Really. They're fake, but they look just like the real ones. They even move and make noise like real ones. You'll love it."

"Okay."

"Which ride are you going on, dear?" Mom asked. She was holding my father's hand.

"The train," I answered. She and Dad had never been on any of the attractions—they were the types that got sick on hayrides.

"That sounds lovely." Mom patted Angelina on the head. "You have fun and we'll meet you at the exit." She took my father's hand, and the two of them strolled off in the opposite direction.

I turned. Looming in the distance were the desert-colored fake buttes that had always reminded me of leaning piles of dung, and screams that were a hundred teapots whistling. It was my favorite roller coaster in the whole world: Big Thunder Mountain.

It was fast, it was dark, and it was loud.

We started up the path.

"I told you, I don't like fast things."

"It's not a fast thing, I swear." I tugged her along. She resisted, but weighed less than tumbleweeds.

I bolted past the sign that welcomed me to Big Thunder…Population 38 and towering boulders sprouting grass and daisies. A couple of rusted wagon wheels tilted against a fence. There were barrels with old milk cans, gnarled trees, a working water wheel, and a Western town. She finally slipped out of my grip near the weather-beaten saloon and a storm-stained assay office.

"I am *not* getting on that!" She stomped her foot and yelled—and then she realized that people in line were staring at her. She stopped and put her head down, meek as a…not exactly a lamb. More like a whipped horse. Either way, a guy in a red kerchief and suspenders herded us between two wooden fences. A large gold "2" was painted on the platform beneath my feet. I looked at Angelina and suddenly thought of the bucking bronco pens at the rodeo.

It smelled like wet metal and chlorine. A recording of an old man warned about hats and wild rides. Then there was the *hish* of steam as the blood-colored steam engine *U.B. Bold,* trailed by open cars the color of desert suns, halted and unloaded its cargo of flushed, breathless tourists. I stepped down into the seat and slid over, patting the cushion. "Come on!"

Angelina looked left and right. I'm certain she was wishing someone would say she was too short to ride and pull her out of line. But no one did. She startled when the lap-bar came down across her waist. Nervously, she extended her spindly arms and clenched the Jesus bar on the back of the seat in front of us.

We took off with a jerk and whipped into a tunnel. I reveled in the *thrum thrum thrum* in my muscles and the *clickety-clack* as we ascended through a hale of agitated bats, fang-like stalactites and seething pools of phosphorous. Angelina shrieked like she was being burned.

I thought of ground-up chocolate and melted juicer tops. I thought of her nasty glares. I thought of my stolen bracelet. And I laughed. "Open your eyes! You're missing this!"

She refused. She shrieked and caterwauled so that it drowned out some of the ride's sound effects—the howl of a coyote, the puffing of geysers, the *churn-glutch* of mining equipment.

And then she dug her nails into my hand, and it hurt. It dawned on me that Mom was right. This *was* acting out. In fact, this was *mean*.

And I was loving it.

Then I remembered the thing I'd used as bait. And there it was, surrounded by empty crates of TNT and poised on a rocky outcropping: the shaggy gray and white mountain goat. He bleated in greeting even as he chomped on the large stick of dynamite he had clenched between his teeth.

"Look at the goat, Angie!" I sneered. "Look at the goat!"

I didn't think she'd do it. But Angelina opened one eye, and then another. Her lips parted in surprise and then spread into an expression something like delight. She loosened her grip on the bar and reached out, as though she could touch it. As we came out from under the shadow of a slapped-together trestle, I saw tears on her cheek. In the sun, they gleamed like fool's gold.

With bullwhip suddenness we dropped and coiled around to the right. Angelina kept her eyes on the animal until we raced through another tunnel. She yelled something, but she may as well have been singing into a dust storm.

We slowed down and rolled past the other end of the town we had seen in the beginning. The Golden Nugget Dance Hall proudly displayed its flag, and an empty noose swung in the breeze. A decrepit baby carriage sat on the front porch of the fake El Dorado Hotel.

I looked at Angelina. Her mouth was set in an angry pucker.

"I want that goat," she said through clenched teeth.

I was so shocked I laughed. "You can't have the Disney goat. Are you kidding?"

"NewMom and NewDad said I could have anything I wanted, and I want that goat!"

"But it's a *computer*, it's attached to the rock. It doesn't *come* off, you stupid bitch," I said.

"You wait." She wiped tears from her cheek. "You wait, because I am going to get that goat, and when I do, he's gonna blow you up!"

Cold fingers worked their way from my neck to my waist.

The ride ground to a stop, and Mom and Dad weren't too far from where we disembarked. They did *not* look happy.

Mom rushed to Angelina's aid. "Oh, baby, it's okay."

"You," Dad gripped my arm, "are in a lot of trouble."

"How *could* you?" Mom pushed her sunglasses up on her head so I could see her eyes, burning like small coals. She rummaged in her quilted hobo and pulled out a paper bag. "Here, Angie. Why don't you have a piece of celery. It'll calm you down."

I watched as she peeled the leaves off the top of the stalk and offer it to Angelina. But instead of taking it with her hand, Angelina bent over and snatched it away with her mouth.

She swatted at a bug on her flour-white cheek as she chomped on the stick of celery. When Mom and Dad turned their backs to start the walk down the exit queue, she glared at me with her strange pink eyes and murmured, "Boom."

Miss Reyna Gets Her Comeuppance on Flash Mountain
(a lost ghost tale of Uncle Remus)

If you've ever been on Splash Mountain—that ride in the Magic Kingdom that takes you through the adventures of Brer Rabbit—you know that when your log boat starts it plunge to the Briar Patch, they snap your picture so they can sell it to you. If you've ever Googled 'Splash Mountain Pictures' on the Internet, you know the rumors about ladies lifting their shirts so they're topless in the picture are true—there are websites that call the place, 'Flash Mountain.'

Disney does its best to keep those pictures out of sight. And that's why they're not snapped by a machine. There are Cast Members whose *whole job it is* to snap the pictures and erase any that might show skin before the guests can see them. Two Cast Members who do that job are Brer Jim and Miss Reyna.

Miss Reyna knows that Brer Jim's smuggling the dirty pictures to the Internet, because sometimes when the shift's over, he walks funny, like he's trying to hide something in his pants. Besides, he's always more eager than a bear chomping berries to take his turn at the photo switch. She's thought many times about tattling on him, but he could make trouble for her because he's got dirt on her, too: he knows she's *real sad,* she'll never ride any of the rides, and she never smiles. And those are all things you shouldn't do when you work for Disney. So even though she thinks Brer Jim is nasty, she never makes a peep.

Now she's not sad because she minds looking at topless girls; it's nothing she doesn't see in her own mirror. She's sad because at least once a day she sees a child puke. Some kid has too much popcorn and up it all comes on the way down the big fifty foot drop, and it's in the picture. Miss Reyna, you see, feels real guilty about the last time she puked she'd rather stick her head into a hopping-mad hive of bees than puke again.

Miss Reyna used to have a twin sister, Amber, and both of them liked wild rides so much they'd hock their dolls if it meant unlimited tickets for one of those sway-you-up-and-around Rainbow rides. When they were twelve, the sisters went to the County Fair, and they had their eye on the Zipper—if you've never seen one, it's a big spinning boom with a bunch of cages somersaulting around it.

But when they were about to get in line, Miss Reyna suddenly felt a strange twitter in her tummy— it was *fear*. But she knew she couldn't tell her sister the truth. Because her sister would laugh at her, and because Mama always told them those kinds of feelings are of the Devil. "Amber," she told a great big lie, "we're not tall enough to go on that ride."

"Poo!" said Sister Amber, "you're nothing but a big goof! That sign says we're tall enough!"

Miss Reyna spied a log flume ride. "Wouldn't you rather go ride on that? We'll get nice and cooled off at the bottom."

"Are you *chicken?*" Sister Amber said, pulling

on Reyna's arm. It was like a tug o' war so fierce Miss Reyna couldn't pull away.

They waited in that long line and got closer and closer to their turn. Miss Reyna knew the only way to stop them from getting on was to tell Sister Amber the truth about her feeling, but she just kept seeing her sister laughing—and a good punishment from Mama—and she kept her mouth shut.

The carnie opened the door to a bright green cage. Miss Reyna decided right then and there she was going to spill the truth, but when she opened her mouth, she let loose her funnel cake all over Sister Amber and the inside of the cage before the carnie even had a chance to strap them in.

Sister Amber was mad. "I can't ride alone. Now you ruined it!"

A boy in the crowd stepped out. "I'll ride with you," he said. "But put us in that hot red car because I'm not getting in that green one that's all full of barf!"

Miss Reyna started bawling as she watched them board the car. She ran as fast as she could to get behind the chain link fence, and that Zipper started up, clickety-clacking and whirring and groaning. She watched the red car and was sure she could hear Sister Amber's scream over all the others. And then against all that clickity-clacking and whirring there was a *hum-whoosh* and a *snap!* And she watched as the red car detached from the boom and hurtled through the air like a piece of blown tire on a speeding 18-wheeler. It slammed into the Ferris Wheel and sparks shot like bullets.

Miss Reyna closed her eyes tight, and when she re-opened them all around her was smoke and twisted metal. She looked at the Zipper. The car she'd puked in was still hanging from the boom, safe as you please. But the red car, it was in the center of the keeled-over Ferris Wheel, just a black husk in the center of a raging fire. Miss Reyna saw a hand-shaped shadow inside.

Sister Amber was dead.

When Miss Reyna got home, the first thing she did was shove every picture of her and her sister in a drawer, so she'd never have to look at Sister Amber. Then she vowed never to go on any kind of ride again. But as her life went on, she still felt amusement parks calling to her, and soon she couldn't resist. So even though the thought of getting on a ride stuck terror in her very soul, and every time she saw a kid puke her heart crumbled like stale bread, she went to work for Disney Parks.

* * *

One day Miss Reyna's sitting in the air-conditioned tree stump at Splash Mountain, taking the pictures. For awhile, everything's smooth as beat cream—no topless ladies, and she doesn't miss a snap. But then one picture comes up, and there's something mighty strange about a girl in blue.

She's got no…*face*. It's just a big blurry smear, like egg whites before they're cooked, and a couple of brown stains where the eyes should be.

For the first time since that day at the County Fair, Miss Reyna gets that twitter in her tummy. She shuts her eyes tight, and opens them again, thinking she's being silly. Because after all, the *other* people in the picture, they're all just fine—a girl in a princess crown, a guy in Goofy ears, a man in a Davy Crockett cap. And in the next two pictures that come up, everybody in the boat looks normal. She tells herself it was probably just a smear of something on the camera lens, and that twitter in her tummy was probably just the chicken strips she ate for lunch, because she thought they might have been a little undercooked when she was eating them.

She keeps on working, until, about the length of time later it takes to bake a strawberry rhubarb pie (because the lines at Splash Mountain are always real long on a hot summer day), she sees another girl come up in the picture, this time riding with a whole different group of folks in a completely different boat. Just the same as in that first picture, everybody else looks just dandy—there's a guy in a tie-dye shirt with his hands up and his mouth wide open, and a couple of little ones hugging each other for dear life. But same as before, there's a girl with her face all smeary. And she's got those oil stains for eyes, and they're starting to spook Miss Reyna.

Much as she doesn't like it, she gets out her walkie-talkie and calls Brer Jim. He's working down at the photo preview station. That's where all the pictures she snaps come up on big screens and folks make note of their picture number so they can take it to the counter and spend their $12.95 on a couple of 5x7's of them screaming their heads off.

"Something's happening in the pictures," she says.

"Oooohh," he says, "what ya got? Good stuff?"

Miss Reyna rolls her eyes. "I think there's something on the lens. Can you go check it?"

She knows he's going to try to convince her to go check herself, so he can sit where she is. Sure enough, his voice is slick when he answers. "How about I come up there and *you* can check?"

"Brer Jim, if you don't do what I say, I'm gonna let the world know what you're up to."

Brer Jim doesn't feel like having a fight over the walkie-talkies, so he does what he's told. "It's all set," he says after he climbs all the hundreds of stairs on the inside of Splash Mountain to the camera perch and cleans the lens. "There's nothing on there."

Miss Reyna furrows her brow. "Are you sure?"

Brer Jim is annoyed. "Sure as I know you were crying at work yesterday, so maybe you should trust me."

Miss Reyna feels like that's a threat, so she turns down her walkie-talkie so she can't hear it and goes back to her work. *Snap, snap, snap.* All the pictures are coming out just right.

Then it happens: another smeary face. Right in the front seat of the boat.

Now she *knows* there's nothing on the lens,

and she starts to wonder if maybe there might be something wrong with the camera—you know, chalking it up to what her Mama liked to call "'possums in the attic." So instead of deleting the picture, she saves it and makes a note in the log book so she can show the repair folks the next day. But just as she's done, and about the length of time later it takes to bake a batch of cookies (because it's just about dinner and folks are heading to Pecos Bill's for burgers instead of waiting in line, so it's getting shorter and shorter), there's another smeary face. And the length of time later it takes to pop popcorn, there's another smeary face. And another. And another. It's got a rhythm to it. And Miss Reyna knows there isn't a camera malfunction that matches up with how short the wait time is.

Miss Reyna suspects Brer Jim is playing a trick on her.

But in some way, she's been tricking him, too. You see, if you let the picture go by and you don't push 'approve', the guests never get to see it. And she was so tangled up with snapping and studying those pictures, she didn't approve even one, and she didn't *tell* him she didn't approve even one. So she doesn't know that Brer Jim has a whole truckload of angry guests down at his booth, wanting to know where their pictures are—never mind that he's pretty sure he's missing out on lots of nakedness—and he doesn't have any excuses to give.

He bangs on the door. "Open up, Miss Reyna! What the hell ya doing in there?"

Miss Reyna wants him to know she's not falling for his pranks. "I know what you're up to, Brer Jim, and I'm not gonna stand for your swindling!"

"What do you mean?"

"The pictures!"

Brer Jim sure wants what she's got. He changes his tone. "What pictures would you be talking about?"

"You know what pictures, don't you lie! I know you're up to all of this!"

Brer Jim's confused. "I don't get it, Miss Reyna. I wasn't up to anything."

"You and some girl are trying to make me think that folks with no faces have been riding the mountain to try and spook me out of my wits so you can sit in here instead of me and watch for nudies all day. How are you doing it? Putting one of those ponchos on her head?"

There's silence from the other side of the door, so Miss Reyna opens it.

"We have a deal, Miss Reyna. You hush, I hush. Why would I want to get your goat?" Brer Jim says.

But Miss Reyna is mad. "Here, you sit in this chair and you tell me it's not you doing it."

Brer Jim thinks maybe she's snapped, so he does what he's told and plants his butt in the seat.

Miss Reyna scrolls back through the pictures on the screen until she comes to the ones with the big old smear where the girl's face should be, and she blows them up real huge on the screen.

"Look," she says. "I think what you're doing is sick, Brer Jim, and I'm in my right mind to go tell Disney Parks what you've been doing with the dirty pictures."

Brer Jim feels helpless as a skunk in a trap—because he doesn't see *anything* out of the ordinary. He scratches his chin and looks at the pictures. He looks at Miss Reyna, whose eyes are blazing. He looks back at the screen and squints. Then he looks back at her. "Where…*where* is it?"

"You lie like a rug!"

"But there's nothing there," he squeaks. "The picture's normal."

"That's it, Brer Jim. Our deal is off!" Miss Reyna leaves the tree stump and slams the door.

"Wait!" He clambers to try to stop her. "But… I mean, I *can* see it, I *can* see it, Miss Reyna!"

But she doesn't hear him lying because she's already racing down the stairs, which are real loud with the sounds of the doom music just before the big drop, where Brer Fox is telling Brer Rabbit "Maybe I'll just have to *roast* ya!" She bangs out the door into the sunlight, into a crush of folks coming out of Splashdown Photos.

And suddenly she spies the girl in the blue dress: Miss Empty Face, just her back, heading toward the line to go for a ride on Splash Mountain. Miss Reyna decides that if she can't get Brer Jim to confess, she'll get the girl that's been helping him.

"Wait!" Miss Reyna yells, but Miss Empty Face is moving fast, ducking around corners and behind folks in the crowd.

Miss Reyna is so busy tailing Miss Empty Face she doesn't realize how narrow the path is getting. She doesn't realize she almost trips twice on account of the floor, which is all bumpy and full of ruts because it's made to look like it's been hacked out of Georgia clay. She doesn't realize she's pushing past people in white rain ponchos. She doesn't see the portraits of Chick-A-Pin Hill and Brer Goose, the shadow diorama of Brer Frog, the WANTED posters for Brer Fox and Brer Bear, or the sampler that reads *Some Critters Ain't Never Gonna Learn*.

And worst of all, she doesn't see the big sign that says FIFTY FOOT PLUNGE AHEAD!, so she's more stunned than an ant hit with Raid when she stops all out of breath at the very tippy top of Splash Mountain, where folks board the boats.

Miss Empty Face is climbing into a log.

"Stop that boat!" Miss Reyna yells.

The Cast Members running the ride just look at her like she's a headless turkey. Miss Reyna knows she can run all the way down the stairs, out the Chicken Exit, and come all the way back up on the other side to meet the girl when she gets off the boat—but if she doesn't get back fast enough, she might miss her forever.

She knows she doesn't have a choice.

She's got to ride the whole ride and catch the girl at the end.

Miss Reyna starts feeling that twitter in her tummy, but she swallows it, thinking only that she's got to get rid of Brer Jim, she's had her *fill* of that nonsense, and so she sets her mouth in a firm little line and steps down into the waiting boat behind the one that Miss Empty Face is in.

The boat grumbles and rumbles its way into the water, and Miss Reyna is suddenly struck with the terror of what she's done, because there isn't *any* way she can get off the ride now. Miss Empty Face is sitting in the last row of the boat in front of her, so Miss Reyna focuses on her yelling to make her fear go away: "Hey! Girl in the blue dress!" she calls. "Wait for me at the end of the ride! I just need to talk to you!"

But Miss Empty Face doesn't even acknowledge Miss Reyna.

Maybe it's because, Miss Reyna thinks, Splash Mountain sure is a noisy place. There's a whole bunch of croaking frogs, singing geese, and drumming porcupines, and Miss Reyna is sucked into the wonder all around her. She breathes in a nice, cool mist, and she sees Brer Bear and Brer Fox trying to set a trap for Brer Rabbit, and over her head she sees possums giggling about going to their Laughing Place. She sees Brer Frog and Brer Gator relaxing at their fishing hole, and Brer Rabbit hopping away across the hills in search of adventure.

But then her boat rounds a corner and there's a couple of twin baby bunnies doing their chores, and it reminds her of Sister Amber. In her heart, she feels something like butter melting, and she starts to cry because she remembers all that crying and screaming in the night for Sister Amber to come back, crying and screaming to God or Brer Sun and Sister Moon to let her relive that day at the County Fair so she can set things right. She cries and cries and begs once again, *Sister Amber, please come back, I didn't mean it.*

Before she knows it, she's at the bottom of the big ramp that leads to that ever-so-familiar fifty foot drop, and it's so steep she's flat on her back looking straight up at the sky. She wonders if this is what it's like to be dead—she's heard that folks who died and come back say they were looking through a long tunnel. Toward the top, she sees Brer Fox's got Brer Rabbit in his clutches. Poor Brer Rabbit's all tied up in front of a big fire, and Brer Fox's laughing, saying over and over "maybe I'll just have to *roast* ya!" Miss Reyna feels that twitter in her tummy, getting worse and worse, and she shuts her eyes tight.

Something colder than popsicles grabs her left hand.

She opens her eyes.

There, sitting right next to her in the seat, is Miss Empty Face. Only she doesn't have a smeary face anymore.

The face she's wearing is Sister Amber's.

Miss Reyna is so happy she doesn't know what to say, but Sister Amber just smiles. "It's beautiful, isn't it, Reyna?"

Miss Reyna looks. They are way up in the air, and the front end of their boat's sticking halfway out over the drop—they've got hang time, is what it's called, and Miss Reyna can see the whole Magic

Kingdom, the heavenly white spires of Space Mountain, the golden roofs of Frontierland, the gleaming top of the Contemporary hotel. All of it sparkles like diamonds in the setting sun.

Miss Reyna, she says, "Yes, it sure is pretty!"

Sister Amber says, "So, are you still a chicken?"

Miss Reyna says, "I'm not chicken any more."

Sister Amber takes Miss Reyna's hand. "Then I'll show you a thrill," she says. "You stand up, and it's like flying on the way down. We get nice and cooled off at the bottom."

Miss Reyna stands up straight as you please.

* * *

Brer Jim sees the whole thing. He sees Miss Reyna's boat come to the edge of the cave just before the plunge. He sees Miss Reyna stand up. He sees her raise her arm in the air and put her hand in a fist like she's holding a baby's rattle. He sees her leap right out of that boat and plunge to her death.

But when the police come and he shows them the picture he took, there is something he's *never* seen on Miss Reyna's face before.

A big old *smile*.

87

All This Furniture and Nowhere to Sit

My wife Elaine drains her fourth glass of wine and there's trouble in her eye-shine.

"Imagine, JJ!" she beams. "We'll be able to sit in an original 1964 Small World boat that was at the World's Fair. It's coming all the way from Disneyland!" She reaches for the bottle and pours herself more. "Disney *himself* put his stamp on those!"

Lainee has always spent most of our money on Disney stuff—pins, every animated classic ever released, stuffed Aristocats and Tinkerbell jeans; in the last couple of years it's gone to more expensive stuff for the walls—signed lithographs, limited-edition sculptures. It's nothing I can't handle. I don't mind the house being Disney-fied.

But I'm *not* into Small World. When she has a little too much wine she puts that song on repeat, and I'm hearing singing dolls to the drone of my electric toothbrush and the pop of my toaster for weeks afterward. Which is not only creepy, but stresses my weak lungs. Having this thing in the house will put me at increased risk. "Where are we going to put it?"

"We'll put it down in the basement, in the play-area," she says of the room where we watch all our movies and mess around with board games. She lifts the glass to her lips.

"What's wrong with the couch?"

"That thing? Come on. We already decided

we were going to get something new."

"A new *couch*." I get up and go to the refrigerator. The photo of us on Splash Mountain is too heavy for its magnet, and every time I open the door it slips closer to the floor. "As in, what's not plaid at Polaris Discount Furniture."

"I've already won the auction." She blows out the candle and gets up from the table. "I can't very well send it back."

I move the photo up higher, but it just slides again. Even though I'm sure she just spent thousands of dollars we can't afford, I don't ask her how much it cost. I'll find out when I see it on the bank statement.

And then I'll keep my fingers crossed that spending this kind of money isn't going to be an ongoing thing, because my chest is already feeling a little pinched.

* * *

The delivery men arrive, looking like beekeepers minus the hoods. I watch them as they slam open the truck's back gates, hover around it, talk with their hands. When they finally figure out how to off-load the boat—turning it on its side, with one guy spotting in the middle and resting his hands on two of the tops of the bench seats—it's larger than I'd remembered. It's about as long and as square on the front end as Pop's bass fishing boat, but twice as wide. I sigh. Not only will the couch have to go, but probably my prized black leather easy chair, too.

Unsure of their footing, they tenuously make their way up the ice-covered incline to the front steps. Their strained expressions tell me they wouldn't stop even if my front door was still closed.

"It's turquoise!" she exclaims as they shuffle in, the boat's side scraping the porcelain tiles. "How perfect! Right down here!" And she claps her hands together and motions to the basement door.

A bottle of wine and a viewing of *Island at the Top of the World* later, she's passed out in the ride vehicle, her legs cockeyed, her head right down against the front seat's nubbed surface. I think she can't be comfortable, but when I try to wake her up, she doesn't move. I would carry her to bed, but because of my lungs it's not a good idea. So I leave her in the playroom. I make sure I leave the lights on and the movie's menu on continuous loop.

* * *

Pop died of respiratory failure in a hospital, cold and away from the farm he loved.

I sat there for nearly two hours after he'd taken his last breath; I meant to call the doctor, but I just couldn't move. Finally, I was about to get someone to come and pronounce him dead when my mother showed up. So she thought he was still alive when she patted his hand, which must have been so cold by then, and said, "Royal, can you hear me? Can you hear me? We have nice plans," she said, "we're all going to Disney World when you wake up."

Obviously this wasn't happening. But even

if he *were* going to wake up, Pop wouldn't go there. When I was eight, the other kids came back from school vacation bragging about their trips to Disney World. About how their fathers gave them ice cream for breakfast and let them get behind the wheels of hot rods on a miniature speedway, crazy jalopies that wound through dark rooms narrowly avoiding oncoming trains—*I was driving for real*, my friend Russ said, *it was so cool, I can't wait to drive a big car!* But when I asked Pop when we were going, when he was going to show *me* how to drive the cool cars, he just kept pulling on the cow's udder and asked, "Jerry-o, why the hell would you want to go *there?* Don't let those kids fool ya—it's a cheap glitzy place. You don't get more there then you do at the county fair, you know. Besides, you don't need to drive a toy car. In a year or so I'm going to teach you the tractor so you can do the lawn. Isn't that better?"

Before I could protest, my mother opened the screen door and yelled, "Roy, the pipes in the bathroom busted again!"

"I'll fix it, Rose-sweets," Pop yelled back.

But he never did. It was 1985, and we didn't have flush toilets that winter.

* * *

Lainee spends lots of time on a Disney attractions collector forum called WareMouse and constantly babbles about her new strangely-named friends, *polynesiandreamergirl* and *20K-4-EVA*. She gushes about their collections and how creative they are. "Somebody made a mirror out of one of the 20,000 Leagues portholes. Is that not awesome?"

I have the checkbook open. The Small World boat was about five times what I thought it might have been—the price of a good used car—and now I'm trying to decide whether or not we can put off the electric and the property taxes (at eighteen percent interest) for a month or two.

Halfway through juggling I realize I'm wheezing, and go into the drawer to pull out my inhaler. I take a puff.

"I thought of something interesting we could do with the boat downstairs, you know, add cushions or whatever, but…I think it'll probably just get crushed by the competition." She goes into the refrigerator and pulls out a glass bowl overflowing with grapes. I close my eyes tight and try not to get dizzy as the medicine tingles in my lungs.

"…new thing." She pours a glass of seltzer. "We just got a piece of a retired Mark IV Monorail! The pilot's cabin! And I gotta tell you *ustillgotwings72* is so jealous right now? He was the only one I was bidding against and he really wanted it. But he doesn't have plans for it like I do."

It takes me a second to register what she's just said.

I pivot in the chair. "What?"

"I told you, he doesn't have plans for it like I do."

"Did you just buy something *else?*"

She shrugs. "It's not like we're poor. We haven't even touched the cash from selling your Dad's land."

"And that money is *not* to be touched."

"Why not?"

"How much was it, Lainee?"

"Cheap. A piece of Monorail Red went for twice as much in 2002."

"*How much was it?*"

She pops a grape in her mouth. "Fifteen," she grumbles.

"Fifteen hundred?"

She tears a bunch of grapes from the vine and throws them in the bowl. "No, thousand."

"Fifteen *thousand?*"

"*Cheap*," she reiterates as she wanders out of the room with the bowl of grapes in one hand and a glass of seltzer in the other. "Besides, wait 'till you see!"

I sit there, trying to swallow. Trying to breathe. And just as I start to think some additional temporary work might be an option to get through next month's bills, I need my inhaler again.

* * *

The delivery men are the same guys as last time, and I pity them as they struggle to get an eight by twelve egg-shaped cockpit through the upstairs slider that leads to our master bedroom.

"Don't come in here!" she chimes after they leave. "I'll let you know when it's safe but I have a lot of work to do!"

I settle into my favorite easy chair in the living room and listen to the sounds of her padding about, moving things. After about an hour I think I'm wheezing again, but when I focus on it, it sounds almost musical.

I'm not wheezing. There's faint music coming from somewhere.

"Lainee?"

"Yeah?" she yells back.

"Are you playing music?"

"No!"

Maybe, I think, it's from the neighbors next door. I decide to go down to the basement, where we keep the beer, and grab a Corona.

But as soon as I get up, Lainee calls me from upstairs.

* * *

The bedroom has mutated. My nightstand is gone. In its place is a podium-looking thing with a snake-necked office lamp attached to it. Taking up most of the wall is the Monorail cockpit—an ovoid cabin with an elliptical windshield and a crescent-shaped bench with bright blue cushions: like a window box. She's rammed our California King bed inside it, so the bench acts as a headboard, and the windshield is like a skylight over where we sleep.

Lainee is stretched out on the bed, wearing a black negligee. She runs her hand over the bedspread. "I've always wanted to do it on the Monorail."

"I've *never* wanted to do it on the Monorail."

"Oh! Come ON."

"How am I supposed to sleep with a window

over my head? I'm gonna feel like people can look in. And I can't put my glass of water on that—podium-thing. It's slanted."

"You should be happy to have the pilot's console right next to you. And I'm going to cut into it to make a cup holder. I just didn't have time to do it now." She laughs, then leans over and grabs the bottle of champagne by the neck. "Here," she says, pointing it at me bottom-first. "Make yourself useful and open this."

I pop the cork while she presents a pair of Mickey logo flutes.

"Where are the other glasses?" I ask of the ones we've been using since we got married. I actually liked them—they had a thick black and silver border around the top, very noir.

"Oh," she says, holding the glasses while I fill them. "I gave them to Goodwill. We don't need them anymore."

* * *

The champagne glasses are not the first of my possessions to be disposed of without my permission. When I was five, I got this thing called Green Kitty for my birthday. It was a pillow in the shape of a cat's head and it had red jeweled eyes. It was only a stuffed animal that sometimes ended up in the corner or under the bed. Until I was nine.

And I saw *him*.

The farmhouse I grew up in had a ghost in it. It was a ghost of an old man, and one night I woke up and he was standing at the window, peering toward the icehouse. I thought it was my father, even though Pop had large broad shoulders, and this man had a curvature in his upper back. "Pop?" I said, but there was no answer. "Pop, what are you looking at?"

The old man looked at me and his eyes burned yellow, and then I heard him laugh, raspy, the squealing sound of slowly letting air out of balloons. He said something but I couldn't hear it. I whipped the covers over my head and implored him to *go away go away*, but instead I heard footsteps toward me. He sat on the edge of my bed, and it was like the pressure of one of the barn cats. Then after a few minutes, he was gone.

After that, I carried Green Kitty everywhere. If I didn't, I heard the old man in the mornings when I made toast and in the middle of the night when he followed me to the outhouse. I saw him lurking in the peony-patterned wallpaper. And Pop wasn't happy with his burgeoning adolescent lugging around a stuffed cat face.

One day, Green Kitty disappeared.

And the old man came back.

I couldn't tell my mother or Pop. They were fundamentalists and didn't believe in ghosts. When someone died he went to heaven. He was out of touch with you, he was gone, and perhaps you'd see him again in forty years, if you behaved.

* * *

A delivery truck blocks the garage, and the same guys are once again making their way up the now-muddy incline—it's been warm and everything's melted, the grass underneath the ice a matted tangle. They are carrying a large blue and silver…car. It's square, with two cushioned benches on either side.

"What are you," one of them huffs as he tries to check his footing, "opening your own amusement park?"

I smile. "For you, admission's always free."

The kitchen has already been dismantled. The free-standing bar is in the living room, and its matching stools are crammed together in the corner like lily pads on a pond. The dinette table has been taken apart and is leaning against the couch. Meanwhile, these blue monstrosities have moved in—there's one against the back wall, another pushed up under the windows, and she tells the men to put the third one in the breakfast nook. It looks like a diner with bright blue booths.

I cringe. "We talked about this, Lainee. We're already behind on one car payment." I think of my Jeep. "This really needs to be the last time."

She's bought light-blue colored Formica-topped dinette tables and is wedging them in between the two benches in the cars. "They were a bargain."

I can feel my chest tighten. "They might repossess a car if we don't get on the ball."

"Pish," she says. "I have more than enough in my IRA, you know that. Just take it from there."

"Lainee. That is retirement money. Not play money. We get penalized every time we take some out."

She walks by me and goes to the kitchen,

opens one of the cabinets, and starts pulling out pots and pans. "Damn, I wish I hadn't gotten rid of the bud vases. Now I'll have to use these milk glass things and they're too big for the tables."

A hand squeezes my heart. I know what bud vases she's talking about. "My *mother's* vases? The cut crystal ones she left you in the will?"

She's pulling stuff out: T-Fal frying pan, muffin pan, juice pitcher, frosted glass wine decanter. "Yeah. She gave us eight, and I was pretty sure I didn't sell them all on E-bay, but now I don't remember."

I lean against the counter. My knees are weak. I can smell the sweat in my armpits. "*You sold my mother's fucking bud vases?*"

The clamor she's making stops. She looks up at me. "She told me before she died she had no attachment to them and encouraged me to sell them. So stop it. And we got enough to cover that pocket watch you wanted so bad for your birthday. The gunmetal one? Remember that?"

Yes, the watch. I did really want it. And it was pricey. And Lainee had done a nice job on the engraving, too.

"Ah. Here they are." She pulls out a set of four milk-glass vases. They're tall and thin and shaped like the famous swing ride at Coney Island that I've seen on all the postcards.

She hums as she rinses the vases in the sink and leaves all the pots and pans in the middle of the floor. As she passes me, she kisses me on the cheek. She sets the vases down, plucks white silk flowers from a gray plastic bag, and makes small arrangements, setting each one in the center of a table.

"Now," she says, taking a step back. "Doesn't that look *great?*"

I heave a sigh. "What are these?"

"These," she says, "are cars from the WEDWay Peoplemover. Well, not really, it hasn't been called that since the eighties or something, but, you know, I'm a purist, I hate the idea that they call it the Tomorrowland Transit Authority now, TTA. Ridiculous. It sounds like a subway system. How very ordinary."

"It looks like a diner in here."

"Doesn't it? Isn't it funky? Imagine when we have dinner guests."

"Yes," I say. "We can sit in different corners of the room and scream our conversations back and forth."

"Let me tell you, this has never been done," she says. "We'll have a good chance. It's going to blow *tomorrowlandtaylor*'s stupid Flying Saucer toilet out of the water."

I'm wheezing again.

I need a drink.

I go down to the basement. I flick on the light and catch the turquoise blur of the Small World vehicle in the corner, sitting in front of the television like a row of empty theatre seats.

I hear children laughing.

I look over in the direction of the Small World boat. Nothing there.

I rub my eyes. "JJ, you're just spooked," I tell myself, attributing it to the upset in my kitchen. I open the refrigerator and pull out a Corona, but I have to thrust my head all the way back and rummage around, because Lainee's cavalcade of fruit waters and a bag of powdered Dole Whip mix blocks my stash.

That's when I hear the music. Again.

I pull my head out of the refrigerator so fast I smack it on the top shelf. Three sodas and a bottled water crash to the floor with a fatal *pluck/smack*, and soda sprays everywhere. I dash up the stairs and slam the door.

My wife doesn't even look at me. She arranges bright blue placemats on the tables in between the seats of the WEDWay cars.

"Were you playing…Disney music or anything just now?" I ask.

She hums a tune I don't recognize as she trims the stem of a white rose, puts it in a bud vase, and sets it on the table. "There. That looks great, doesn't it? Charming." She turns. "I'm sorry, did you say something?"

* * *

I *did* finally go to Disney World, by the way. With Lainee for my thirtieth birthday, and it came on the heels of my telling her the sad story of how I'd never been.

She stopped twirling her fettuccine on her fork, her mouth forming an O. "That's terrible and just cruel to say that to a little boy," she said. Then she began pushing the food around her plate. "Just awful."

"He probably had a good point," I took a sip of my beer. "I think it's just one big marketing machine."

"You can't say that if you've never been."

Three weeks later, she presented me with a huge box covered in Mickey Mouse wrapping paper. Inside, there was a Birnbaum's guide so I could choose which restaurants we were going to eat at, a Magic Kingdom map, and a pair of Mickey ears.

When we walked into the Magic Kingdom she was so happy she cried. She hugged the "mayor" of Main Street and marched us straight to Adventureland, because, she said, most people with the little kids hit Fantasyland first and so the lines at Adventureland are shorter. She didn't need a map. She moved through the crowds with the innate navigability of a mole.

I was looking for that sense of rip-off glitz Pop had said was rampant.

But it wasn't there. I found clean streets and small details, music to match each land we were in, flowers that were in such perfect bloom they looked fake. Nathan's hot dogs and real Dole Whip pineapple ice cream. A palace of leaded glass and topiaries in the shapes of animals.

We had lunch with a pack of princesses. Saw Lincoln speak at the Hall of Presidents. Ate a turkey dinner that would've rivaled Pop's at the Liberty Tree Tavern. And rode in those hotrods I had dreamed about. In front of us, in an aqua car, was a toe-headed boy and his father. And I thought of all those lost father-son days we could have had, doing things other than slaughtering chickens (which really don't run too much when they have their heads cut off— it's the turkeys you have to watch). And I felt that same betrayal you feel when someone has died and you find out a deep secret about him.

* * *

Even in the dark, I can see my reflection in the Monorail windshield above my head. I move my hand, and watch the shadow move with me. I roll my head from side to side, and the shadow moves with me. I lift my arms and make a shadow creature. Cow, shadow cow. Dog, shadow dog. Rabbit.

Nothing appears.

Rabbit.

The shadow doesn't move with me. It goes the opposite way, and then I see the outline of a *face*. A face peering back at me.

Oh dear God it's the man with the yellow eyes and no Green Kitty

"Ack!" I sit up and smack my head on the slope of the windshield, gasping for breath. I yank the water glass from the cup holder Lainee's since cut for me and wing it at the figure.

"What?" Lainee snorts awake.

My chest wrenches. "I saw someone!" I throw off the covers and set my feet on the carpet, but it feels gritty. Like it's seeded with crumbs. I grope around on the ridiculous podium-thing, pilot-console or whatever for my inhaler. "Someone was looking down on me through the windshield!"

"It was just your reflection," she says.

I puff on the inhaler, let the mist fill my lungs. I peer up at the windshield. There's nothing there now.

Lainee reaches for my arm and pulls me back down into the bed and curls me up against her, and I smell the scent of orange in her hair as I watch my reflection for the smallest change.

* * *

I stand in my kitchen. What I need to do is get a beer, cram my body into one of those WEDWay diner booths, and open all the mail, which includes this month's bank statement. What I need to do is convince Lainee to stop this.

I stand in the doorway and consider the new living room arrangement. Lainee bought eight of the ride vehicles from something called If You Had Wings that I've never ridden. They look a little like satellite dishes, and when they first arrived they had front panels with safety bars that lowered toward your lap. Lainee's removed the panels, laid the things on their backs, and glued them onto these white stands. She's put giant pet cushions on the insides. Essentially, she's converted them into papa-san chairs, and they form a neat circle around a coffee table she's made out of a dark blue oval with the shape of an airplane cut into it.

Everything that had been in the room before—the frosted glass coffee table with the chess board inlay, the entertainment center with my collection of 1930s ashtrays and detective novels, even the *television*—is shoved in the far corner in a heap, blocking the lower half of the window where our Christmas tree is usually displayed.

Jesus.

I sigh and choose a papa-san. I close my eyes and listen to the house. Upstairs, a drawing bath. In the kitchen, the ticking wall clock and the *clunk-whoosh* of the ice maker. In the living room, rain pattering on the skylights.

you could widen your world if you had wings

Somebody *said* that. That wasn't me thinking it. And it was…a whisper. A raspy—

you could do many things

I scramble from the vehicle and glare at it. "You can't scare me anymore!"

you can do all these things

I take the stairs two at a time and burst into the bathroom.

My God. Lainee's finished replacing the tub with a Skyway vehicle, a bright red Jacuzzi-depth box with a corresponding metal shade umbrella.

"Christ!" She drops her *Orlando Attractions* magazine in the water. "Don't you knock?"

I can't speak because I'm trying to breathe. It's like someone took my lungs and made them smaller, squished up the bottom half. Finally, I manage, "Stop this shit, Lainee!" I blurt. "The stuff you're buying is…haunted. Possessed. Or something."

"What," she says, her mouth smashed into a little red line as she retrieves her magazine, "is wrong with you?"

Water drains from the soggy pages into the tub.

"You know what? I know exactly what's wrong with me."

I slam the door and hurry downstairs to the living room, where, damn my lungs, I drag those huge ugly papa-sans—which don't fit through the living room entryway—out through the side sliders to the porch. It takes me two hours, but coffee table, entertainment center, ashtray collection, television, leather couch and all, I put the whole room back the way it was.

*   *   *

On the farm, Pop was up before the sun, doing chores. When I was five, I started chores too, small stuff like feeding the chickens. Then I'd go in and my mother got me dressed.

"You have to learn how to tie your own shoes," she said, waving her finger like my ignorance was going to land me a spot in whatever circle of hell it is for traitors of kin.

One particular morning we were supposed to go to the farmer's market—it was my first time—and I scrambled to get my shoes on.

"Your father's leaving, Jarrod Jason," my mother called up the stairs.

I struggled with the shoes. I just couldn't do

it…was it left over right, right over left? I couldn't remember.

"Hurry up, your father's leaving," she repeated, and I heard Pop murmur something, something like he had to go, I guess, because then I heard the door slam.

I sat on the cold wooden floorboards, crying because I missed it. Pop had left without me.

"You can go next time," my mother soothed, but I was inconsolable. I ran down the stairs to the front window, looking out at the cow pastures and the smoke puffing from the milk house chimney. I thought if I just wished hard enough, the ratty truck with the crooked front fender would be rumbling its way back up the road in a cloud of dust, coming back for me.

* * *

Today when I get home from work, the living room is back the way it was.

That's it. I give up.

I decide to take a ride out to the Dairy Queen. Or, *screw that*—to the nearest bar.

I go out to the garage, and my car isn't there. Instead, there's a bright yellow bumper-car sized jalopy with a tall wheel in front of the driver's seat.

Jesus.

By the time I get upstairs my throat's dry and my lungs feel coated with fur. Lainee's brushing her hair.

"Where," I gasp, "the hell…is my car?"

107

"Parked out in front of the house." She rises from the vanity, goes to the closet, and sheds her robe.

I sink onto the edge of the bed. "Why is that other thing parked in my spot and not yours?"

She pulls out a neon green dress with orange polka dots. "'That other thing' is one of the cars from Mr. Toad's Wild Ride. Isn't it adorable? It was a steal—they were having a clearance, because the only place that ride's left is in Disneyland and they have what they need out there. These are all the ones left from when they dismantled the one in Disney World in 1998." She wiggles into the dress and stands with her back to me. She looks like a big highlighter. "Zip me?"

I do.

"And it's parked in your spot because I have the convertible. Your car can take the weather." She reaches out and takes my hand, then touches my hair. "I wanted to get something for you, for a change. I'm not going to do anything with it. You can pretend you're going places. Do you like it?"

The room is spinning a little bit. I think of where I left my inhaler.

"I'm going out to that collector's reception," she says. "I'm taking the photos of all our great new furniture with me. I'm pretty sure we're going to win the prize."

"What prize?" I remember the inhaler's in my pants pocket and reach for it.

She sets her hands on her hips. "The

WareMouse Forum prize for 'Most Creative Use of Old Attraction Equipment'. I told you about it."

I put the inhaler in my mouth, hold my breath, then let it out. "You did?"

"Yes." She takes a bright pink handbag off the dresser, unzips it, and shoves a lipstick and a compact inside. "That day you were bitching about the Monorail, but I've mentioned the competition stats to you a couple of times. Where've you been?"

She blinks at me, waiting for my answer. I loosen my tie and whip it free from under the shirt collar around my neck; suddenly I'm hot and I feel like my shirt is soaked with sweat.

"Do you want to come?"

"No," I say. "I think…I'm going to rest."

"Good." She kisses me on the cheek. "You've been looking a little piqued lately. Wish me luck!"

After the sound of her car dies away, there should be silence, but instead there's cacophony. That damn singing I heard the other night, geese quacking, bagpipes, hyenas laughing. Whispering: *you could follow a tradewind, you could catch fish.* Other sounds I haven't heard before—repetitive doorbell chimes. Wind whistling, distant voices. Low rumbling. The walls of the house shake.

I take a breath and my lungs don't fill, don't fill enough. Something squeezes my chest, my throat closes up, my sight is a hail of tunneling silver flashes. The Monorail bed. The Wings cars in the living room. The WEDWay midget diner in the kitchen and dining room. The Skyway tub in the bathroom.

The Small World boat in the basement.

I have all this furniture and nowhere to sit.

"STOP!" I gasp as the world goes dim.

* * *

Quiet. It's dark outside.

"Lainee?" I call out, but there is no response.

I can breathe, even though there's a wheeze every time I inhale. I close my eyes and focus on it, where is the wheeze coming from, is it lower in my lung or higher up, or is it in my throat? It's coming with every inhale, but I can't feel it. I can't feel *where* in my lung it is.

Then I realize it's not me.

That noise is a car horn, in metronomic rhythm. And it's not Lainee's car horn; this is an old bicycle horn, a silly New Year's Eve noisemaker. I remember the jalopy in the garage.

Oh, shit.

Enough, I decide. *Just enough. I am going down there, and I am telling whatever the hell this thing is to get out of my house.*

I sit up and creep down the stairs. The horn hasn't stopped, and it's coming from behind the garage door at the end of the hallway.

That's it. Now. Go.

I fling open the door and plunge forward, howling like I'm scaring away bears at a campsite although I know my throat's so damn dry it's probably coming out as nothing more than a squawk.

There's a dark figure in the jalopy's passenger seat.

I stumble back into the hallway and slam the door, listening to my own breathing as it gets louder. I hear footsteps in the garage, coming closer. They stop on the wooden step.

I press my ear to the door to listen. I hear breathing.

"What do you want?" I cry.

"Jerry-o," someone says.

There is only one person in the world who ever called me that.

"Pop?"

The doorknob jiggles a little, and I reach out to hold it. The jiggling stops. I turn the knob and open it, and there he is, sitting in the jalopy, his hands on the wheel. He motions me over.

He pats the front seat next to him, and I get in.

Skeletons in the Swimmin' Hole

"He did it," my husband says.

It's so dark I can't see his eyes—we're at the Polynesian Resort's Spirit of Aloha Dinner Show, and they're about to dance with fire so the lights are off—but I know there's no expression in them anyway. He's in a trance. "Ohhhhh."

David channels the last thoughts of dead things. Back home in Baltimore, the ability's onset has forced him to end his taxidermy practice. Recently, though, he's seemed to get better.

I heave a sigh and reach for the carved coconut monkey head that holds my Pele's Fire Punch, put the straw in my mouth, and drain the drink.

He finishes reading the air and sets his hand on top of mine. "I'm sorry, Cora. I know this is a vacation."

"I just didn't think there'd be any dead things in Disney World, that's all. You were clean for almost a month. I was hoping—"

"I know." He puts a square of pineapple bread on his plate next to a pile of chicken bones.

The drums begin, and a limber man in a grass skirt twirls a flaming baton.

* * *

The flashes started on David's fortieth birthday.

We were celebrating at the Annabel Lee

113

Tavern, and the waitress had just set a quarter duckling in front of him. He looked at me as though he was going to say something, but then his expression went blank. He turned his gaze upward.

"What?" I twisted to look and noticed writing painted high on the wall: *Till they sorrowfully trailed in the dust.* There was more to it, but it wrapped around a corner where I couldn't read the rest. "That's from a Poe poem. I don't think that line's from 'Annabel Lee.' I *want* to say it's from 'Ulalume.'"

But he didn't answer.

"David?"

His eyes moved as though he were reading from a page in the air. "Why did she leave me alone? Why?"

I leaned closer to the table. "David? I didn't leave you alone. I'm right here."

"She left me!"

He hadn't mentioned his ex-wife, Helena—who had left him for another man—since just before our wedding two years ago, but that was the only 'she' I could think of. I reached out and gripped his wrist. "Helena left you, David. I didn't."

"No!"

Everyone in the tiny place went quiet; there was only the mournful *Firebird Suite* Berceuse floating from a speaker in the ceiling.

"No!"

My face burned under the stares. The flame from our table's candle snuffed out.

"I can't get out!" David shouted.

I released his wrist and turned to the pair of women at the next table. "I'm sorry…my husband is…I…"

The waitress, panic in her eyes, approached. "Everything okay?"

I shook my head. "I'm…I'm so, *so*, sorry, I don't know what's going on, just bring us some take-out containers and the check. Fast."

She nodded and rushed off.

"I can't get out!"

"Yes, David, you can. We're going out. Right now."

Outside, the rain had turned to sleet. "Where is she?" David yelled. A couple walking across the street stopped, and then ran. "Where is she?"

"Stop it!" I screamed. "You're scaring me!"

"She left me here!"

"I did not! Helena did!" Sleet stung my cheeks.

He was quiet for a moment; in the distance, I heard sirens. Then he blinked, marveling as though he had no idea how he'd gotten outside. "Cora?"

"I'm right here." I was relieved. "I'm right here, I'm not going anywhere, and what Helena did to you will never, never happen again."

He reached out with trembling fingers to touch my cheek. Then he fell against my shoulder and cried.

When I wrapped my arms around him, I dropped the take-home containers. His duckling fell out and rolled into the street.

* * *

We undressed and got into bed. On the ceiling, the shadows of tree limbs were bony fingers; at the window, the sheer curtains were ghosts.

David sat up and read the air again.

"It was poison." He got out of bed and left the room.

I sat up, turned on the light, and followed him. "David?"

He stood in the hall in front of my photographs; I specialize in dead animals. Carcasses and skeletons. I like to try and capture the almost human qualities of an animal frozen in its moment of death. Four poster-sized prints of mine lined the upstairs hallway, ones that had recently won awards and garnered me a contract with a small Baltimore publishing house. A coffee table book of my work—*Skeletons in the Closet*—was due out in a couple of months.

David set his palms on the photo of a bird skeleton sprawled at the base of a bathtub. "I thought it was food. It was poison."

It gave me the chills. "Wake up. You're having a nightmare."

But he moved down the line to the next one: a bear skeleton in a tutu, left behind to die when a long out-of-date zoo had been closed. "My heart hurts. Why did they leave me here?"

I remembered that bear's cage. It had been unlocked. Not broken open, not rusted, but unlocked. Which means the bear probably could have wandered off, as the rest of the animals in the zoo had done, but for some reason, he never did. He was…

…broken hearted. He died of loneliness.

David wasn't having a nightmare.

Was he somehow sensing these dead animal's *last thoughts?*

Impossible.

"What are you seeing, David?" I asked. "What are you seeing? What are you *hearing?*"

He moved down to the dead fox.

I grabbed his hand. "Enough. Please, stop."

He continued to search the ether for answers, but then I figured out what I could do.

I set my hand on his crotch; he was hard as a rock.

He jolted out of it. "I'll make it up to you."

And he started to, with his hands up under my peignoir set. He was the old David within a few strokes, the old David when he ran his tongue over my navel, the old David when he gripped my hair and entered me.

But it didn't last more than five minutes. He went soft, rolled away from me, and started to cry again. When he'd finished, he said, "I'm closing my practice. Tomorrow."

I sat up and looked at him. "What? Just like *that?* I mean, this could be just a freak thing, a…"

"No. It isn't. And don't take photos anymore. Don't bring that stuff into this house ever again."

"Ditch my *life's work?* Are you kidding me?"

"I said no more!" he shouted.

He'd never raised his voice to me. Not once. I

threw off the comforter, stepped into my slippers, and grabbed my pillow. I lay on the living room couch and flipped on the news. After a commercial for Ajax, a reporter in a plum-colored suit was talking about a pet store fire in the Canton area. By the time the firemen got there, all the animals were dead.

The Canton area. That was the same section of the city as the Annabel Lee Tavern; I had a dim memory of outside, saying something about Helena, *hearing sirens.*

I groped for the remote control and turned up the volume. "It's really sad, and the owner, I don't even know where she's at right now," said a red-capped neighbor whose breath came out in puffs. "It was just too late."

I remembered what David had said at the restaurant: *Why did she leave me? I can't get out! Where is she?*

The animals in the pet store were dying. And he'd heard them.

It was true.

I went upstairs, took every one of my skeleton portraits down, wrapped them in brown paper, and shoved them in the basement.

* * *

"So you want me to stop the presses on this book? Because I can't. We've got tons of preorders," said Michele, who ran the small house that was publishing *Skeletons*. "Besides, if he's closing his practice you guys are going to need *some* income."

We were having dinner at the Blue Sea Grill, and I was putting more emphasis on the fine wine than the food. I stared at my so-far untouched Blue Sea Crab Cakes. The accompanying limp tangle of julienne carrots turned my stomach. Michele, on the other hand, chowed down. She ate when she was stressed. She was armed with a plate of linguine, so I broke the news. "I promised him…I wouldn't take any more photographs."

Michele dropped her fork. "You're not serious."

I sighed. "I am."

Michele picked a mussel out of her pasta and set it in her salad bowl; she'd forgotten to tell them sans mussels on her order. "Look. Maybe this is like a weird mid-life phase for him or something. Maybe it'll pass."

"I just…I hope so, but I don't think so. Everything is so fucked up. And I have a bad feeling it's going to stay that way."

"Optimist, huh?"

"Some days," I said, "I just want to run."

"Well, maybe you should." She twirled linguine on her fork. "What I mean is, would it be better for you if you left the marriage."

"That would make me as bad as Helena, Michele. I can't do that to him." And anyway, I was pretty sure I didn't want that. I still *loved* him. There was still a David in there, somewhere. His laugh was gone, his sex drive was gone, his interest in *us* was gone…but he was in there, somewhere. "I couldn't imagine life without him." I picked up my fork, but only to shove aside the carrots and poke at the crab cake. "It's not his fault."

"Just make sure you don't compromise your integrity." Michele broke a piece of garlic bread in half. "That's what people don't understand about integrity. People think it's all about 'doing the right thing' even if it's bad for them. Are you going to eat your carrots?"

"No."

"Great." She reached over with her fork, stabbed a heap, and moved them onto her plate. "What people forget is that *true* integrity is doing the right thing while doing what's best for you simultaneously."

I summoned the waitress and ordered more wine.

* * *

At home, all was dark. "David?"

The only response was murmuring coming from the second floor; it ceased, then started again.

I ascended the stairs and worked my way down the long hallway, snapping on lights as I went. The murmuring grew louder as I approached the bathroom door. I put my hand on the knob and turned.

He was in the tub, naked, reading words from the air. "It's a long way down. Moon looks different from here."

Something crashed and fluttered against the bathroom window. Startled, I rushed over and pulled back the curtain.

There was a pigeon between the dead mini-roses in the window box. Its wing was cocked at a strange angle; it shuddered and then went still.

I caught my breath and yanked the curtains closed. "David—" I was going to try to break him out of it, but when I looked down at him, I was disturbed to see his penis was harder than it had been in weeks.

I remembered when only *I* could do that to him.

* * *

The signing event for *Skeletons in the Closet* was at the Barnes and Noble, in a renovated factory in the Inner Harbor.

That was where I met Ted.

The event was on the second floor in the section devoted entirely to Poe, which was out of immediate eyeshot due to the building's twin smokestacks. He was the only one waiting at my table; he stood tall and confident, but his oxford shirt was unbuttoned to almost the navel, and he wore no T-shirt underneath. He was so thin his collar bones were pronounced, and in his equally bony hands, he clutched a copy of *Skeletons*.

"I think," he said, "the bird on the windowsill just got cooked from laying in the sun too long? It was like he'd finally found some peace, like he'd been freezing his ass off all this time and he was finally warm, and he just let himself die there."

I blinked. Most of the time, fans only wanted

to tell me all about their own photographic adventures and prefaced them with innocuous comments like "I love your work." Not only was this man very specific—the photo he referred to was the smallest one and was buried at the back of the book—he didn't utter another word.

And that's when I was struck by his eyes. They were amber. I didn't know if the color was from special contact lenses or if it was natural, but either way, it was exquisite. "Are you a photographer?"

He shook his head. "Where did you take that photo?"

"An abandoned Borscht Belt hotel in upstate New York four summers ago."

He leaned closer as he set his book on the table; he smelled like fresh-brewed coffee and dusty attic. "Make it out 'To Ted, Love Cora'."

I grabbed my green Sharpie and did as I was asked. It was like I watched myself from outside.

He picked up the book but kept staring at me. "I hope you're going there again, soon. It was just such a ripe place for you."

My cheeks flushed. "Oh, I…no." I looked down at my row of Sharpies and started to neaten them up so their caps were even. "I…I'm not shooting skeletons anymore. This will be my only book on the subject."

Something heavy filled the room.

"You can't be serious."

"I am."

We stood there until a teenager approached

the table; her black tank top depicted a pink preying mantis over a red heart. She pulled four copies of *Skeletons* off the pile.

He reached out and seized my wrist, and his touch sent an all-consuming need through me: I *wanted* him.

"It was nice meeting you, Ted. Would you excuse me?"

"Would you meet me after this for a drink? Six o'clock? At The Horse You Rode In On?"

I heard myself say *yes*.

* * *

By the time we finished our sixth glass of amontillado my lips tingled. I was definitely drunk. And Ted's amber eyes were more powerful than they'd been at the bookstore.

He ran his finger around the rim of his cordial glass. "Wasn't your husband David a taxidermist? Best one in the city, I read an article a couple of years back."

"He doesn't do that anymore, he stopped." I drained my glass and slid it to the edge of the bar.

He was silent for a long moment, then furrowed his brow. "Why not?"

I motioned to the bartender for a refill. "He had a little bit of an accident, I mean…incident. Incidents. He heard animals' last thoughts."

The bartender nodded and re-tied his apron, and as I watched him get me a fresh cordial, a low roar started in my ears. Which meant it wasn't a good idea for me to have another one, but it felt so good going down, and Ted—Ted had clean, soft-looking skin, and a freckle that looked like a spot of brown sugar near his right ear.

The bartender set the drink in front of me. I sipped it, but for some reason thought it needed a bit of zest. "Can I have a women…I mean a lemon wedge?"

"I didn't think animals had thoughts," Ted said.

"I didn't either but it's totally true." I felt dizzy, and I closed my eyes. Someone in the kitchen dropped a dish, and the noise was followed by mumbling—people talking, but I couldn't make out what they were saying. I imagined what it must be like to hear the animal's thoughts as David did. "I wonder what they sound like, though. I never asked him about that."

The bartender put down a bowl of lemon wedges. Ted picked up one and squeezed it into my drink. "So you didn't want to stop taking pictures, did you? He wanted you to?"

"He made me." I shot back.

Wow, I thought, *that was angry.*

But Ted wasn't fazed. He smiled and leaned closer to me. He smelled differently than he had before—now, it was like soap and dirt after rain, and I was sure he was the type that'd never ask me to give up anything. I looked at Ted's freckle and imagined the taste of his skin.

"Why?"

"Because he also hears what they're all thinking in the things…" My mouth was so dry. "I mean the pictures. Not things. Sorry. You know, what they were thinking when they died. What the animals were thinking when they died."

"Would you ever go back to it?"

I lifted my glass to my lips and sipped; the drink's temperature was so cold I could feel it through the glass, and it occurred to me that my fingers hadn't hit the shutter button in so long that they actually ached. "I'd…I'd lose David if I did."

Ted stared at me until I met his gaze. He quickly looked away and squeezed a lemon into his drink. "The sex is that good, huh."

"Excuse me?"

"The sex. The whole sex and death thing. I read somewhere that most people are horny after funerals or near-death experiences. All that death he hears? He's gotta be horny all the time."

Yes, he is, I thought. But we hadn't had sex in months. He was only erect when he was in communion with dead things. *But not for me. Not anymore.* For the first time I noticed stubble on Ted's cheek, and I wanted to touch it, I wanted to take his shirt off and caress his chest.

Ted leaned closer and put his mouth near my ear. "This is so gonna sound like a pick-up line, but do you wanna get a room?"

I thought about integrity, and my visceral response was *no, I want to fuck you right here.*

* * *

Three days a week, Ted banged me so hard he could have ground my bones to powder. On Memorial Day weekend there was a freak frost; Ted and I had cancelled our picnic, and instead were going to shack up in a high-rise over near Westminster. I'd packed a few things, a new peignoir set and some shampoo, and went to toss the bag in my trunk.

A mouse skeleton was curled up in the spare wheel well.

Feeling uneasy, I looked about the street. No one had a key to my car, not even David. How had the mouse gotten there?

Something inside me said, *take its photograph.*

I stopped for a second. I promised. I promised I'd never take another dead-thing photo, I promised David, and I'd managed to keep my promise for several months. All I had to do was get a trash bag and dispose of this poor thing and move on.

I looked at the mouse again. It had a strange innocence to it, the way its paws were curled up near its snout, like a fetus.

Ashame, I thought, *ashame to waste this moment. It's only one photo. It's only one.*

I cast my gaze up to the second floor of our house; I could hear the bathroom exhaust fan running, which meant that David was in the bathtub. I went back inside and up the stairs; I pressed my ear to the bathroom door to be certain he was in there.

"It's cold," he said. "It's cold."

I wasn't sure if he was talking about the mouse, but it sounded like it. I shuddered, because the image of him erect while having visions of a dead mouse was more than I could bear at that moment.

I tiptoed up the second flight of stairs to the third-floor darkroom, where I'd dumped my camera. It was sitting on the shelf, where I'd left it, covered in dust.

* * *

After that, it was like God killed things where I could find them. There was a dead bird on the hood of my car outside Eddie's supermarket. A stench led me to the grass by the old railroad station, where I found an almost-skeletal dog. Nellie, one of the kids that lived across the street, ran over screaming because her mother wasn't home and there was a rabbit carcass on the sidewalk.

I couldn't help myself. I photographed them all.

* * *

Two weeks later at the Sheraton, Ted and I had finished making love. He smoked a cigarette, lay on the bed on his stomach, and surveyed all of the most recent photos I'd taken that summer.

I sat on the floor, wrapped in a white sheet. "You know," I said, "I just don't see the same…sense of natural desperation in these photos as I did in the ones for my book." I sipped from a mug of coffee we'd used the in-room maker to brew. "It's like…I dunno, there's something sort of…staged, or fake, or hollow about these animals."

He took a drag. "What are you talking about?

127

I think they're fantastic. That one of the dead cat at Edgar Allan Poe's monument? Wow. Fucking wow."

There was something disturbing in the way he said the word *fucking*. It wasn't violent, not really, but it seemed he put a little too much emphasis on it for some other reason. The word hubris popped into my head, though I didn't know why.

"Yes, but," I said, "how did it get there? I mean, it doesn't look…right. How does a cat just pick *there* to die and no one does anything about it?"

"Who cares how it got there. The photos are still sad. You're the queen of unacknowledged death. You should love them." He stubbed out the cigarette in the ashtray. "I know *I* do." And then he rolled over on his back and touched himself, and I forgot all about it.

* * *

The day things changed was just after the last leaf had fallen from the trees. David and I sat at the kitchen table, eating beef pot pies around a cinnamon-scented candle.

He lifted his fork halfway to his mouth, and then dropped it. It plopped into the center of the pie, and a spot of gravy rocketed into the air and landed on a stick of butter. Behind him, through the slider, a crow alighted on the porch railing.

I held my breath, waiting for him to slip into a trance.

But he didn't.

David had a strange fire in his eyes; he got up from the table and leaned over—knocking the candle to the floor—and kissed me firmly on the mouth. Forks, napkins, and food went flying, and outside, the crow watched David take me right at the kitchen table, hard and fast and noisy and blissfully painful.

When we were done, we did it again.

I decided to end it with Ted.

* * *

I pulled into the Papermoon Diner, a place so busy and crammed with crazy-odd decorations Ted and I met there often because no one was going to spot us in all that chaos.

Ted hadn't seen my car pull up. He stood on the sidewalk and smoked a cigarette near an old toilet, sink, and bathtub the diner had transformed into planters.

I cut the engine and watched him in the rearview mirror as I put on my lipstick; then I remembered that the day's rendezvous was the sort where the wearing of lipstick might send the wrong message.

I climbed out of the car, and he waved.

Funny, he looked thinner than he did when I'd last seen him.

He went to kiss me on the mouth, but I turned my cheek at the last minute. There was a flash of alarm in his eyes. "What's up?"

"We have to talk."

He frowned. "Why?"

I shook my head. "Over French toast."

A waitress with a T-shirt on that read BANG ME ROYAL seated us beneath a collection of He-man action figures that had been glued to the ceiling; it was near the front door and the grill, for which I was grateful—it would make a hasty exit much easier.

I skimmed the menu, trying to decide if I really did want the Big Dipper French toast thing or if today's occasion required the heavy grease of a good old simple Moon Burger.

"Coffee," I said.

Ted shook his head. "Nothing for me, just the water's fine."

I put the menu down. I'd decided on a Moon Burger.

He reached for my hand. I pulled away. "I can't see you anymore, Ted."

He didn't react; then he got that little smirk at the corner of his mouth. "Oh, come on, Cora. What did I do?"

"Nothing. I just can't see you anymore. I need to break this off."

Anger flickered in his amber eyes. "You don't mean that. The sex is great. You're not getting anything like that at home."

"Ted, listen—"

"After all I've done for you. Getting you back into your work. Giving you a second book on a platter."

I frowned. "What do you mean?"

He didn't respond immediately; BANG ME ROYAL set a coffee in front of me. "Ready to order?"

I opened my mouth, but Ted told her to come back in a few minutes.

"Hey," I said, annoyed. "We're adults, and this is over. Stop acting like a child."

"You owe me. All those skeletons. The bird. The cat. The rabbit. The dog. You think you found all those by accident? I found those for you. You… didn't want to go out looking for the art anymore, so I brought the art to you. That's all."

"What?" I heard my own voice trapped inside me, like my ears were clogged shut. My stomach knotted with the realization that *he had done all of that.* He had christened my car with the dead bird, put the dead cat in front of Poe's monument, dragged the skeletal dog from God knows where. *He'd terrified my neighbor's little girl by leaving a dead rabbit in front of her stoop.*

His eyes were full of hope.

I fought the bile creeping up my throat. "Ted. No. I'm done."

He glared at me. His bottom lip trembled. Then he stood up and hurled his water glass at the wall. It crashed into a random doll—He-man's Skeletor character. The figure plummeted to the floor, and its pale blue leg shot up onto the counter. "Hey!" shouted the bear-like, spatula-waving cook.

Ted raced to the door, shoving aside BANG ME ROYAL, and was gone in a slam. A couple of antique Pez dispensers dominoed off the cash register in his wake.

For a moment I felt like I wasn't in my body. I

touched my wrists, my forearms, my thighs, my chest. Yes, I was still there, still intact.

BANG ME ROYAL had caught her breath. She came over and set a hand on my shoulder. "Are you okay?"

I wasn't sure. It was the oddest feeling, like I was all skin and no bones.

* * *

Over the next three weeks, David did not have a single flash.

Then the smell pervaded the living room: like rotted bananas, rancid meat, and dog shit. I knew that smell, and I knew what it meant: some animal had died in the walls.

It had happened when we'd first bought the old row house. We'd had to live with the smell until the creature had completely deteriorated—we certainly weren't going to start sledge hammering the place to try to find it. It had been an inconvenience for a few days.

But this was panic time. This thing of David's, this thing that had mercifully *stopped*, was it triggered by something, like an allergy? What if he came home, smelled the decay, and we were back in la-la land? I fished out every reed diffuser I had and went nuts with sugar plum and autumn spice.

David came home. "It smells in here."

"Yeah." I rummaged in the freezer for the Chicken a la King Lean Cuisines we were going to have for dinner. "I figured I'd…freshen up the place."

"No, I mean, like something *died*. You're not fooling me, honey. You think I wouldn't know the smell?"

I closed the freezer door and set the dinners in front of the microwave. I heard the *ca-chunk* of his extending the recliner, the rustle of his newspaper; I waited.

Nothing happened.

I ripped into the ends of the dinner boxes and slid out the meals; then I heard him set down his newspaper and get up from his chair.

"Stuck," he said.

Oh no. I shut my eyes, afraid to look. *Please, please, please let me not see what I think I'm going to see. Please let me not see him reading stuff out of the air.* I took a deep breath and peered around the corner.

He was on his hands and knees in front of the fireplace, peering up the chimney.

"David?"

He turned and looked at me with a satisfied gleam in his eye, a gleam I hadn't seen in awhile. "No, honey." He got up off his knees and brushed his hands on his jeans. "I mean, I really think something got stuck and died in the chimney. I only smell it when I walk by the opening. It's nowhere else in the house. I'll call the sweep tomorrow."

I tried not to heave a visible sigh of relief.

* * *

On Friday, JOEY from Chiming Chimneys of Baltimore showed up. After he'd been working for a while, he rang the front door bell. He held the carcass of a giant bird.

"Look at this, ma'am. You need to have a cover on that chimney. Poor thing prob'ly tryin' to make a safe nest for its little ones, you lit a fire, it burnt up like a nice crispy chicken at the KFC."

"What…what kind of bird is that?"

He shrugged. "Bird of prey of some kind I think, hawk, eagle, whatever. I've never seen anything like this before, but it's too big to be just like a robin."

The bird was extraordinary. Its wings were only burnt at the tips, and its body was charred in some places and the color of burnt sienna in others. Its blackened beak was slightly open, and its talons were gnarled.

It looked like it had been screaming as it had tried to claw its way out.

I really, *really* needed to photograph it.

And David wasn't home.

"Ma'am." Apparently JOEY was still talking.

"What?"

"I said, you want me to install a cover on there so this doesn't happen again?"

I remembered. "It's got to be up there somewhere, the cover. We just bought a really expensive one and had it installed last fall. You guys did it, in fact."

But JOEY looked confused.

"It's okay," I said. "Just…just put the bird down and finish up, come back, and we'll pay you."

"Ma'am, we're supposed to dispose of the…"

"Look, Joey, you're a nice kid. Do your job."

"I'm really supposed to—"

"Joey. If you want a big-ass tip, you'll do what I told you."

He hesitated, but then stepped into the foyer and put the bird down at my feet. At last he left, and I slammed the door.

I raced upstairs, seized my camera, and got to work. I tapped the bird's legs with the tip of my boot. *Click, click, click.* I gently tilted its head. *Click, click, click.*

"Someone put me here."

Jesus. David was home.

He startled me so much I dropped my camera and accidentally stepped on the bird's right leg. The bone shattered and the leg fell off.

David appeared in the doorway, reading the air. I toed my camera under the foyer table.

"Someone put me here." David said.

I had a pretty good idea who that someone was. I snatched my cell phone and keys, and ran out to the car.

* * *

I drove to the Inner Harbor and parked in full view of the aquarium—somewhere teeming with people—before calling Ted.

"I knew you'd call eventually," Ted said. "I know you couldn't resist after what I did. You need me."

I was so furious my neck was physically hot.

"You psycho. You absolute fucking psycho. Tell me, was it still *alive* when you rammed it in there? And what the fuck did you do with my three hundred dollar chimney cover?"

He just laughed. "Meet me at the hotel."

"Ted. No."

"You want to. You need me for more pictures."

"I don't want you. I don't need you."

The silence was ominous. Then he said, "What do I have to do to convince you?"

"Nothing, Ted. Don't come near my house again." That's when I got the idea. "And if you decide to? Be aware that I'm not going to be there for several weeks. I'm going away."

"But—"

"Go ahead. Do your worst. Fill my house with carcasses. I won't be there to see them. And when I get back? I'll have you arrested."

I flipped the phone closed and rested my head against the seat. The silver tower of the aquarium gleamed against the cerulean sky, and I thought about where we could go. Just David and I. We had to go somewhere where animal carcasses were never, ever allowed to sit for more than an hour. And was there any place in the world that was really like that? I shuddered at the thought of all the unseen dead rats in a big place like New York City, all the dead sea life in the ocean beneath a cruise ship, all the partially-consumed prey on the African savannahs.

But then I remembered our honeymoon. I'd

been disappointed. I'd brought my camera, just in case there were some great carcasses around—death in the colorful, happy place we'd chosen to go would have made for yet another series of award-winning work. But the whole time we'd been there, we'd seen not one dead thing, not even a crushed lizard in the resort parking lot.

There had been no dead animals in Walt Disney World.

I drove home. David and I packed our bags, told both sets of neighbors where we were going, politely asked them to keep an eye on the house, and took the first flight out of BWI.

* * *

I decide what David had said tonight at Spirit of Aloha was just a fluke—perhaps an animal had died somewhere in the vicinity of Luau Cove and David just picked up on it. After all, the Polynesian Resort is lush with tropical foliage; it'd be easy for an animal—something as tiny as a toad—to die and go undetected for a couple of hours. That's all.

When we get back to our room, David surprises me—there are rose petals all over our bed. "Happy second honeymoon."

We make love with the slider open and the scent of palm trees and trillium floods the room.

* * *

In the middle of the night, I wake with a start because David's not in bed. He's a dark figure out on the balcony; the slider is still open, and the white sheer curtains billow in the breeze.

I step out into the night air; below us, Sea Raycers bob in their slips.

"David?" I set a hand on his shoulder. "Come back to bed."

He points out toward the Contemporary Resort. I'd thought they kept the lights on all night, but apparently not. It looms against the indigo sky like a deserted Aztec pyramid.

"Ohhhhhhhhhhh," David moans. "Ohhhhhhh. Make. It. Stop. Let. Me. Go."

He doesn't move, but breathes heavily. Like he's huffed his way up a flight of stairs. "I…can't…breathe…"

I give up and sit on the edge of the bed. The wooden, sinister-grinned Tiki god that serves as the base of the lamp glares at me. I turn its face to the wall.

* * *

The next morning, David is a self I haven't seen in a long time. We sit in 'Ohana, where I'd booked us a brunch reservation without being aware that it was a children's character breakfast. Which means that Mickey, Minnie, Goofy, some other character in a Hawaiian dress and a blue hamster-like thing I don't recognize romp through the room, shake maracas, and rile up over-stimulated kids to a way-too-loud song about roller coasters. They also stop by our table to pose for pictures with us.

But David loves it. He laughs and orders seconds of Mickey Mouse shaped waffles, bacon, eggs, sausage, fresh fruit, and orange juice. I've never seen him eat this much and wonder if all this smiling will induce vomiting.

"Let's mix it up!" David shouts as a parade of children in multi-colored leis marches by, "And rent a boat today!"

I almost choke on my juice. "Really?"

"Yeah!" The big blue thing sidles next to him, and I take a picture. In it, David opens his mouth, sticks out his tongue, and waves a half-bitten sausage.

The thing nods and moves to the next table.

"It's a gorgeous day," he says. "Look at it out there. And this lake is so big."

I don't want to squelch his enthusiasm, but I know for a fact the man has never driven a boat in his life. "Are you sure you know what you're doing?"

He poo-poos me and shovels a forkful of eggs in his mouth. "All the tourists do it. Kids are driving those things. I saw them yesterday, in those Sea Raycers? The ones we can see from our room?"

I know what he's talking about. Tiny speed boats that look like a tad too much power would capsize them. "You don't want to…rent a pontoon boat instead? We could handle that better. They're slower, bigger."

Mickey Mouse arrives. David grins. "Take the picture, finish your juice, and let's go."

* * *

139

Bay Lake glitters like a lawn of shattered glass, so it's difficult to see boats in the distance.

"Is this living or *what?*" David shouts over the noise of the engine. He touches my already sunburned leg, and even though I'm happy to see him elated, I can't say I'm not nervous. This tiny boat is rabbit shit compared to the Magic Kingdom Ferry that runs between the ticket center and the park, cat crap compared to the shuttles that run from the Polynesian, Wilderness Lodge, and Contemporary. Rocketing in between all of those are the pontoon boats full of probably drunk people and a handful of Sea Raycers piloted by children.

"David, be careful!"

But he pushes the throttle down and the thing goes even faster. The Contemporary Resort is behind us now. A land mass is straight ahead. On the shore, a wooden pirate ship is beached; beyond the trees, I can see the damaged roof of a building. The dock at the island's tip is broken, half-submerged under the lake's surface.

I seem to recall that we're not supposed to be anywhere near this island, and fumble for the map the guy at the marina had given us. Sure enough, the area to the right of the island—and to the distant shore, where we're headed—is a RESTRICTED ZONE. "Hey, we need to go more to the left?"

He doesn't answer.

"Honey?"

He reads the air. "Ohhhhhh."

I'm certain my breakfast is going to come up;

I belch and it tastes like orange juice. "David!"

But he's still reading words out of the clear blue sky. His hand pushes the throttle down and we're going even faster.

I remember what the guy at the marina had said: *if you're in distress, just sit and wave your arms and the Lake Patrol will come and find you.*

Well, great. If I could get David to stop the boat. And right now, he's completely gone, repeating *Let. Me. Go. What. Is. Happening.*

A huddle of rocks and timber and overgrown southern pines looms directly ahead. Wooden walkways, stairs and rusted waterslides wind like fat snakes around the trees. We're headed right for an enormous, disintegrating dock. *Jesus, we're going to die.* I unbuckle my seatbelt and lean over to grab the wheel from him, but he fights me. "David, stop it!"

"Ohhhhhh."

Finally, he lets go of the wheel, but it's too late. The boat slams into the dock and vaults clear over it onto a weed-furred beach.

The engine sputters and dies, and I black out.

* * *

When I wake up, the only sounds are the distant pulse of fireworks and my heart.

It's almost dusk. David is next to me, and, except for a cut on his forehead, looks fine. I shake him gently. "Wake up."

He doesn't respond.

"Wake up."

With a snort, his eyes pop open. "Wha…"

"You drove us here. In one of your trances."

He looks around. "Where the hell are we?"

For the first time I look around us. The dock to our right slants precariously, its newel posts angled like scullers. The remains of waterslides separate at their seams. Mangrove trees are corpse-gray: dead. A pair of support beams inside the gazebo fall against each other, like hands in prayer. And a wooden deck that's missing boards flanks a splintered sign that reads ISHING OLE. It smells like mildew, rotting fish, and some other latent odor that's familiar but I can't quite identify.

The place practically wails in despair.

"I think," I say, "it's some kind of…water park. It looks like it's been abandoned." I reach over and unfasten his seatbelt. "The boat's wrecked. We're not getting back to the Polynesian this way." I realize that neither of us brought our cell phones—we'd been afraid of damaging them. "Maybe there's a pay phone in this joint."

He nods. When I try to climb free of my seat, I realize my ankle is swollen.

We hobble up the beach and onto a barrel bridge that surrounds a smarmy green pool of water. Herons, perched on the rope railings, look with initial interest, then turn back to peering into the pool. What wildlife could live in it, I don't know, but every few minutes, a heron dives down and comes back with something in its beak. We pass a rusted trash can with the words Disney's RIVER COUNTRY emblazoned and still readable, though the Mickey Mouse on the logo has been partly scraped away and is missing a face.

Lounge chairs sit in front of a cracked, drained pool; they're poised on either side of an ashtray which still has a few cigarette butts in it. Untended pink geraniums bloom everywhere. There is a nest of disintegrating ice cream wrappers, a few rusted soda cans at the base of a dead tree, and a stiff, stained towel draped over a diving board. A filthy tire swing spins listlessly from a frayed rope.

David says nothing. We move toward POP' PLACE, SNACKS & REFRESHMENTS AS YOU LIKE 'EM. So many weeds and trees have sprung up in the gutters and under the roof shingles it looks on the verge of collapse. Yet it's under that porch overhang I see a wall-mounted pay phone.

"Over there," I say, but I turn and see David is gone.

He's reading the air, and he's walking. He's walking straight for the deep end of the dry swimming pool.

"Let. Me. Go," he says. "What. Is. Happening."

"David!" I run to catch up with him, but it's hard with my swollen ankle. I trip and fall, and my knee smacks on the pavement. Pain radiates through my hips, back, arms.

He's still walking.

I struggle to my feet, hold my knee as stiff as possible, and limp to get to him.

Closer, he's getting closer.

He sticks one foot out over the edge, and I throw myself to the pavement and wrap my arms around his ankles. He teeters, flailing his arms—

—and then falls.

On top of me.

I can't breathe.

"Ohhhhhhh." He gets off me and heads for a large rock that has a tunnel cut through it; it runs under a pair of cracked water chutes that would have emptied into the pool.

"I…can't…breathe," David keeps saying. "Ohhhhhhh."

As we get closer there's a stench of boiling cabbage and rubbing alcohol. I salivate as I do just before I throw up, but stifle it. "The stink," I say.

But David doesn't respond. He's still in his trance.

We duck into the tunnel and see two rooms. One door isn't marked except for the red spray-painted word WHORE. The other door, marked GENTS, has been ripped from its hinges; it rests carefully against the tunnel wall, as though someone plans on reinstalling it later. The restroom's light is on.

"Ohhhhh." David crosses the threshold.

I grip his arm to pull him back, but he breaks free, so I follow. The room's pale blue tiles are stained with mold and mildew and….

…blood.

In the flickering fluorescent light, a gruesome diorama emerges. All around us are piles of bones, little animal bones, big animal bones, birds and squirrels and raccoons and rabbits and God knows what else. Fox carcasses hang from the ceiling. A dead deer is posed with its front hooves in the sink.

And seated on the toilet is a human skeleton.

I don't just scream. I slap a hand over my mouth, hobble clear of the room, and spew breakfast all over the sidewalk. *Ted. Ted did this*, I think as I heave. *Ted did this, and this is serious shit.* He stalked us...*the neighbors, you ass, you told the neighbors, he probably asked the neighbors where you went.* And my God, is he still *around*? Is he waiting somewhere with a weapon? *Did he find all those animals or did he actually fucking kill them?*

I'm shaking.

David is out of his trance. He sets a hand on my shoulder to steady me. He helps me climb to my feet, then pulls over a couple of old lounge chairs. One is clean, and he guides me to it. The other is covered with dirt. He brushes it off with his hand, and sits down.

For awhile, we say nothing. There is the distant sound of the Ferry horn.

"I'm sorry," he says. "I ruined the vacation."

I reach out and pat his leg, feeling more guilt than I can possibly hope to expel.

He stands up. "We need to call the police."

"There's a pay phone. On the wall next to the menu sign at the snack counter. I saw it when you were moving toward the...that..." *tomb? Old restroom?* "...you know."

David sets his hands on his hips. "What kind of person…what kind of person would do this?"

The kind of person that rammed a bird down our chimney. The kind of person your wife was fucking three times a week behind your back.

My arms break into goose flesh. I look up at him and read his expression; he has no idea there's any connection, none at all.

"And what if whoever did this is still here?" He approaches me and brushes a strand of hair from my face. "You're in danger, Cora."

You're in danger. Not, *we're in danger.* Not, *I'm in danger.* But, *you're in danger.*

In the distance, there is the sound of what must be a parade in the Magic Kingdom—Mickey Mouse's voice is unmistakable, even though I can't make out the words.

And there is another sound.

Rustling. Footsteps.

David looks at me, but there is no fear in his eyes. Instead, there is helplessness.

I think about the word integrity.

Acknowledgements

In 1983, Epcot Center opened the future World attraction *Horizons*. The ride took passengers past people dwelling in cloud cities, barren deserts, oceans, and space stations. According to *Horizons*, this was all within reach—we had only to imagine it to make it real.

It is the "we" part that's key here. No creative person, in realizing a dream, imagineers alone. There are people who inspire, guide, cheerlead, and support. I've been blessed with many during the development of *Skeletons*; it couldn't have come to fruition without them.

I'll begin with the gung-ho Disney fan community. Ricky Brigante and his *Inside the Magic* podcast was a fount of inspiration, and the ITM forums members readily shared their knowledge. Thanks to Louise Belmer, Scott Bolderson, Brerfigment95, Kevin Casey, Dean Cottrell (a.k.a. DC1309), Fastlane, Paul Hammond, Alex Gravlin, kirby_is_kyaan, Ed Kuyon (a.k.a. monorailred), Greg Lege, Tracey Morris, Kurt Nelson, raedahlin, Geoff Salt, Mark Silverman, Cassie Thomas (a.k.a. cassiez76), TQM, and Steve Vitale (a.k.a. loosetoon)—most of whom know me as WEDWay Bleu. I was also in constant communication or traveled to Orlando with Disney Park lovers from all over the country: Duff and Gail Bramley, Shaun Burris, Jason Cook, Claudia Cummings, Melissa Duckworth, Madi & Lauren Gagne, Lourdes G, Meghan Guidry, Amberrose Hammond, Jennifer Winston Mayette, Missie Petersen, Bonnie Spittler,

Louis Venezia, and Suzanne & Adam Zuckerman.

I was lucky enough to be surrounded by writers and artists who fostered my growth in new and interesting ways: Brady Allen, Steve Almond, Lynne Barrett, Jody L. Campbell, Chitra Banerjee Divakaruni, Chris Emmerson-Pace, Toni Logan, Jeanne Mackin, Mark Ellis and Melissa Martin Ellis, The Newport Round Table, Antony Galbraith, Walter Giersbach, Emily Heckman, L'Aura Hladik, Stacy Horn, YoungJames Kenny, Susan Kim, Rachel Kovaciny, Pete Lemieux, Tamara Linse, Rob Mayette, Maureen McFarlane, Helen McGarvie, Howard Mittelmark, Sigrid Nunez, John Palisano, Dr. Daniel Pearlman, Rachel Pollack, Lon Prater, Al and Maryanne Profeta, Gerald Rivard, Paul Selig, L.L. Soares, Heather Sullivan, Jonathan Sullivan of LOKI Graphics, Inc., The URI Writers Group, Cynthia Wilson, and Rashena Wilson. I'd also like to thank Marc Bisaha and Melissa Hunt, who aren't only fun to be around, but reminded me that a life without the occasional risk really isn't worth living.

The generous people with whom I work helped keep me grounded; they were always enthusiastic about my work, never stopped encouraging me, and provided me with countless opportunities in many areas of my life—but were also good about reminding me that a life in balance is a more productive one: Rick Balmaseda, Chris Bonner, Janet Cutler, Rob Giampe, Keith Gillotti, Lori Godino, Bill Hall, Kathy Hartford, Robert Hubiak (inspiration for "Doing Blue"), Michele Ingram, Stefanie Ingram, John and Cary Kortze, Brian Magee, John McKee, Diane Nebinger,

Amy Nimer, Steve Pendergast, Craig Polinchock, John Potusek, Chuck Protano, Jim and Pam Riel, Jeff Rubin, Stephen Schneider, Guy Schoepfer, Kim Ursini, Linda Vilardi, and Tanisha Watson. A special thanks to Lisa Patton, who puts up with me every day, and to Charlie and Amy Wilson, without whom a residency at the Norman Mailer Writers Colony— which changed my writing life in more positive ways than I can count—wouldn't have been possible.

Living with me is much like living in the center of a maelstrom, or so I've been told. I'd like to thank Charles Smith, my housemate of thirteen years, for providing a stable yet whirlwind home life. And, of course, Nathan, who has been there for me in all the ways a mate should be—even when I was unbearable to be around. The man has endless patience.

In any creative life there is one little spark that starts it all. I wouldn't be writing today if it weren't for Maryanne Squeglia, who introduced me to horror stories when I was way too young for my parents' liking, and her mother, Delores, who has been reading my stories since I was knee-high. Every time I thought 'I need to stop this stupid writing thing and go be an accountant,' I'd think of their disappointment and I could never quit.

Appropriately, I've a couple of ghosts to thank as well: my parents, the late Charles W. and Linda G. Petersen. They made sure we went to Disney World throughout the 1970s and 1980s, no matter how tumultuous the family environment. They instilled not only a love of the parks, but an understanding that a person can escape the world for a few days, but can never really escape himself—which is what these stories are about. If there's a Polynesian Village in heaven, I'm sure that's where they are.

Horizons was shuttered in 1999 and demolished in 2000 to make way for Epcot's *Mission: Space*. The haunted Disney World series is unlikely to meet such a fate; in fact, there's already a second book in the queue. To take on *Horizon*'s original theme song, *if I can dream it, I can do it*—as long as I have such enthusiastic dreamers by my side.

Kristi Petersen Schoonover
Provincetown, Mass.
August 10, 2010

152

KRISTI PETERSEN SCHOONOVER's short fiction has appeared in *Carpe Articulum Literary Review, The Adirondack Review, Barbaric Yawp, The Illuminata, Full of Crow, Eclectic Flash, Macabre Cadaver, Morpheus Tales, Citizen Culture, MudRock: Stories & Tales, New Witch Magazine, Spilt Milk, Toasted Cheese,* and a host of others, including several anthologies and the forthcoming *Disciples of Poe* from Last Rites Publishing. She holds an MFA in Creative Writing from Goddard College; she's also the recipient of a Norman Mailer Writers Colony Winter 2010 Residency. She hosts the paranormal fiction segment on *The Ghostman & Demon Hunter Show* broadcast, www.ghostanddemon. com, and serves as an editor for *Read Short Fiction, www.readshortfiction.com.*

She also teaches the first ever online course in writing the ghost story (Paranormal Fiction: Grasping the Ghost Story) for To Write Well, *www.towritewell. com.* She lives in the Connecticut woods where she still sleeps with the lights on.

Her website is *www.kristipetersenschoonover.com.*